CROWN OF RUIN

Book Three - Crown of Death Saga

KEARY TAYLOR

CHAPTER 1

I WANT TO BREAK. TO SHATTER. I COULD CRUMBLE, A million pieces scattered across the stone floor.

But there are eyes—so many eyes. Dozens of them, hundreds perhaps. They watch me. They watch their queen.

I've been under their eyes before. I've been studied, scrutinized. I know what they are looking for in this moment.

I can't crumble.

Because right now I have to be queen of them all.

"Get out," I say evenly as I stare at my husband's blank face. My stomach turns. My jaw tightens.

I stand straight. I take one deep breath. I turn to face the masses.

"I want everyone, and I mean everyone save Alivia, Ian, and Eshan out of this castle. But if anyone tries to leave Roter Himmel, the punishment will be one hundred years tied up in the middle of the desert where the sun never sets."

Eyes widen, breaths suck into lungs.

I see it, they doubt me. If I really am the Queen. If I mean what I say.

If I were Cyrus, I'd probably kill someone. Drag them out into the sunlight outside, watch them scream, watch them cry in agony. I would probably tear someone's skin off, inch by inch, while everyone watched, to show them how deadly serious I am.

But I am not Cyrus.

I am Sevan.

"Do you all understand me?" I ask quietly.

No one speaks. They only watch me with wary eyes.

"Do you understand your Queen?" I bellow.

Some take a step back. Eyes widen. Others narrow at me.

"Do you understand if you leave our city you will regret it for the next 36,500 days?" I threaten with an angry tremor in my voice. "Do you understand if anyone tries to travel on silent and dark feet, I *will* know?"

While the majority nod their heads solemnly—most know better than to defy me, others doubt.

I make a mental note of each of them.

Of their own accord, my eyes drift, studying each of those that surround me. The shock of Eshan. The horror of Alivia. And the bitter anger of Ian.

My eyes shift from him to those who look at me with doubt. And I look back to Ian.

He looks over at them as well, and I know he gets my silent communication: *take note of the doubters.*

We may not like one another, maybe we never will, but I know in this, we speak the same language when it comes to being distrustful and suspicious of others and their motives.

Looking back at those who weren't smart enough to take me seriously, I know that some will die.

And I don't care.

Emotion wells in my eyes. Tears threaten to slip down my face.

But I hold them in.

I'll burn every one of them to the ground if it means avenging Cyrus.

"Leave," I let the word quietly slip over my lips.

It starts at the back, bodies work their way toward the main entrance of the castle. The guards are wary. Unsure. They feel they're abandoning the posts they have held for centuries. But with dark, hard eyes, I stare at them.

The great hall empties out, and slowly, the room grows quiet.

As I watch the last of them leave, one tear slips down my face.

I can't breathe.

My chest hurts.

My feet feel like lead, a million pounds each.

But I turn.

Slowly, I cross the space to stand at my husband's side.

Cyrus.

The man in the cage beside me laughs, something low and dark. It rumbles through the room.

"How the tide will turn now that the King is dead," he says. "After all this time, after all our efforts, it was so *easy*."

I feel my eyes ignite red and my teeth grind together so hard they threaten to crack.

"Get him out of here," I growl.

A sound whistles through the air, one I've heard once before. The man in the cage howls in agony. I look over my shoulder to see him holding his neck, a thin needle sticking into his flesh.

It's one of those same darts Rath shot Eshan with once.

Ian steps forward, slipping something into his pocket. He picks up the keys the guard had left on the table, unlocks the cage, and grabs the quivering man by the arms.

I meet Ian's eyes as he drags the man away.

Something in them tells me he knows where he's going, he knows exactly where to take this man.

And I remember; Ian was once imprisoned here at the castle.

I can't think about the past right now. Not when here in front of me, the love of my very long, very broken life, lies dead.

I reach forward, touching my hand to his cheek over a splash of blood.

I can't describe the emotions that rush through me. Relief. Longing. Completion. Utter agony. They pummel me with the force of a typhoon.

But I feel it, even now, looking at his wrecked body —the love.

"Cyrus," I whisper. Just his name pulls at all the strings attached to my heart. I feel them lacing back together with his own. We are bound together, through time.

"There…" a shaky voice says from behind me. I hear footsteps and Alivia appears in my peripheral vision. "There's a chance." Her voice trembles. She sounds terrified. "Before I was brought here to the castle, someone tried to kill

4

Cyrus." I look over at her. She looks down at her King, her eyes filled with emotions. But it is largely pity as she looks over at me. "I watched them stake him right through the heart. I watched him die. But only moments later, he rose again. He was perfectly fine."

Everything in me trembles. I feel like I'm made of a million cracks. They spread, inching out over my skin, and if I move wrong or speak too loudly, I'll shatter.

"It's been hours," I say quietly as I look back down at him. The blood that covered the table has turned black, congealed. "It's been *fourteen* hours."

I feel every one of those seconds since I last heard his voice, and then that wet thwack.

I close my eyes.

Cyrus, I call out into the dark recesses of my mind.

"Cyrus said it once himself," Alivia says. "He cannot be killed."

But there is that huge cavern of doubt in the tone of her voice.

I think back through the ages, through my lives.

"I've seen it before," I say. "Attempts on his life, ones that should have been successful. But never..." I take in a shaky breath. "Never anything like this."

A warm hand covers my shoulder, and his presence forces out five more tears. Eshan leans into me. He doesn't know what to say, what sixteen-year-old boy would? But his presence tells me everything he can't voice.

"I need you two to figure out some kind of security," I say. My eyes rise, drifting around the great hall, not really focusing on anything. "We can't let anyone escape Roter

Himmel. We're severely undermanned right now until we can figure out who is still loyal, but I do know whoever else was tied to this, they're safest to try and leave. Don't let them."

Alivia nods. Eshan's eyes widen—it's such a huge task I've asked of him, especially now that he is merely human. But he steps away, following after Alivia.

It shouldn't take Ian long to secure Cyrus' killer in the dungeon. He'll be able to help them shortly.

I feel numb. I look around, and suddenly realize just how alone I am.

Everything—everything about our world could change right now. Could already be changing.

I've led beside Cyrus for thousands of years. But always —he was King. Always, he was the one who could execute what needed to be done. I never wanted the role of leader. I never thought to take the reins.

But now... Now it is all up to me.

I'll do what I must to keep the kingdom together.

Right now, I have to try. I have to hope.

It nearly breaks me, moving him and seeing parts not attached where they should be, but I have to move him. I gather Cyrus' body into my arms, his head set carefully in his lap. I turn to the back of the great hall, toward the passageway that leads deeper into the mountain.

Through torchlight, I carry my husband's mangled body. Down a long stone hallway. Around a corner. Past the upper armory. Down a spiral staircase.

My feet and my heart know exactly where they are going, though I have never walked this path with this face. This is a place I haven't stepped foot in for over a thousand years.

6

I turn a corner into a dusty and cluttered storage room, filled with books and old suits of armor. I make my way to the very back of the room.

Attached to the wall is a torch holder. There are six scattered throughout the room, but I walk directly to this one.

I reach up and pull on it.

Stone grinds against stone. A cold rush of air fills the room. A small opening appears in the stone.

Careful not to jostle him, I step inside into the dark with Cyrus.

Silently my feet descend the spiral staircase, dropping deeper into the side of the mountain. Above me, I hear the opening grind closed, sealing us inside where no one besides the two of us has ever been.

Down, down, down. We spiral ever downward. I cannot see a thing in the total and utter absence of light, but my memory guides me.

Finally, my feet meet flat ground. Soft dirt. I smell the slightly damp air. Hear water drip.

I blindly step forward, one hand outstretched as far as I can, feeling for the wall.

There, I find its rough surface.

I slide my fingers back and forth. I search, and there, find the latch. I pull, and a rush of cold humidity washes over me.

Stepping through the doorway, I put a hand out, searching for obstacles in my way. Moving carefully, I set Cyrus' body on the table I find, and grope around for the torches. I strike a match, and the brilliant light sears my eyes for a moment.

Squinting against the agony, I take the torch back to its place on the wall.

I inhale the heavy, wet air, and cast my eyes about.

Stone and dirt walls surround me, closing in a space that is roughly twenty feet by twenty feet. The far wall is roughly hewn, sloping off further back, exposing a grotto, so deep and light deprived, it's pitch black.

Along the walls there are tables and shelves. They're lined with instruments and glass vials. Mummified bodies are stacked in wooden coffins against the farther wall. Small creatures and organs float in liquid along shelves. There are books on astronomy, on anatomy. Spiritual texts on God and the divine, hoodoo and voodoo.

In the center is a fire pit and above it hangs a large hood where a chimney works its way to the outside.

It's a mess. There is stuff everywhere, books turned to random pages. Instruments are here and there. Maps are spread out on the floors. There's the body of a wolf against the far wall. The smell tells me it hasn't been dead long.

Cyrus has been working.

Cyrus was always a curious man.

After he cursed us, after we moved here to the castle, he never searched for science and magic beyond what he'd already found. But he never stopped looking for a way to end the cycle of my deaths.

Death after death—through centuries—Cyrus has fought for me.

He has always failed. Because I know: there is no cure for what he did to us.

But he's been here, within the last few days, working. Trying to find a way to break my curse, just like he promised.

I will fix this, he had pleaded.

He's been trying.

The shelves bear many things, but as I walk along them, I feel at a loss. Those bodies won't help me. Those books of prayer won't bring him back.

But I've seen Cyrus work miracles. I've witnessed his methods, seen him heal incredible things.

There is always one common factor, one method Cyrus turned to every single time.

I build a fire in the pit, the thick smoke filling the room as the air finds its way through that long unused chimney. I stoke it, hot and bright and have to shield my eyes against it.

I wait for embers to form, wait for the logs to burn down. I kneel beside the firepit. I reach to the sides of the smoldering logs. Black ash covers my fingers. I spread it to the other side, smoothing it over my skin. Over my palms. Over my knuckles. Up to my wrists.

Ash for renewal and hope.

Turning, I cross the space, back to the table Cyrus rests upon.

I straighten him. Lay out his legs, smooth down his slacks. I place his hands over his chest, and my heart hurts.

I remember what it felt like to have those hands caress my back. Run up my thighs.

I remember every place they've been, on every body I've worn over the centuries.

The air catches in my throat, pain threatening to overtake me. I can't let it. Not right now. Not when I'm his only chance.

Gently, so gently as if he were an infant, I place my hands

on his cheeks. I guide his head back to his neck, to his shoulders.

You've done this before, I tell myself. *Two months ago. You pieced together another person.*

It's where all of this began. The woman who had been attacked by a vampire—no, played with. And soon after, my human, ignorant life was through.

I slip into Logan as I carefully piece the broken and parted pieces of Cyrus together. I smooth his shredded skin. I make it look like there was never anything at all that happened.

I pull my shirt off, up and over my head, using it as a rag, and dip it in the water of the grotto. Returning to Cyrus' side, I wipe away the blood, all traces of what happened.

He lies there, still, peaceful looking.

"Where are you right now?" I ask out loud.

I always speak to the dead. I learn their stories. Tell them about myself.

"Are you in the dark?" I wonder quietly as I clean him. "Or are you in the dreamland I've often found myself lost in? Am I there with you, in our memories?"

My voice echoes here in the cavern. I sound unearthly. My voice is too big, too ancient. Old as the stones.

"Wherever you might be," I say, gently touching his cheek. "I need you to return." I study his eyelashes. I'm glad his eyes are closed.

It was his eyes I first fell in love with.

I can't look in them and not see life, the spark that made him so much bigger than this world.

When next I see them, I want them to be clear, so I can say these words trapped in my throat.

"I need to tell you something," I continue. "I need you to know. I need you to feel it, to see it in my eyes." I place my other hand on his other cheek. I climb on the table, straddling his body. I lean in, my hands on his skin. I touch my forehead to his.

"Return to me, *im yndmisht srtov*," I breathe into him.

He doesn't move. He doesn't open his eyes. No breath gasps into his lungs.

I shift back.

Black is smudged over his cheeks. My handprints are there in ghostly form.

I smear it over his forehead. I relieve him of his shirt, and smear it over his arms, his chest.

"Come back to me, *im yndmisht srtov*," I whisper to him over and over as I smear him in ash. I send out a constant prayer to anyone who will listen. To the heavens. To the stars. To God.

"Give him back to me," I say. "He is mine, and I am his. Give him back to me."

CHAPTER 2

I BLINK OVER AND OVER, BUT THE HAZE DOES NOT CLEAR from my eyes.

Thick gray and purple smoke fills the air. It floats through the field, laces between the trees, blots out the sky.

I walk through the tall grass, propelled forward by...by something. I feel it, and I'm drawn forward. Through the dark. Through the smoke.

I stretch out a hand, hoping to prevent myself from tripping over any hidden objects in the smoke.

Suddenly, there's something hard and warm. Soft fabric.

And the smoke clears, and there are those green eyes.

Those soft lips.

Those strong shoulders.

"Sevan," he breathes. I see relief clear in his eyes. His shoulders relax just slightly. "Good, you are here. I need your help."

My brows furrow as he steps out of my reach. He bends,

picking something up off the ground. He stands again with an armload of wood and strides off into the smoke. Quickly, I follow after him.

He walks across the field and the smoke grows thicker with each step. I cough, attempting to clear it from my lungs, but it lingers, saturating every crevice of me.

"Cyrus," I call out to him, picking up my pace in an attempt to catch up. "Cyrus, I need to talk to you."

He disappears as the smoke grows so thick I can't see more than two feet in front of me. I dart after him, feeling desperate, every nerve in me anxious at the separation. And suddenly, I nearly smack right into him, there in front of me in the smoke. He bends over, placing the wood down, precise and exact.

My eyes widen as the wind shifts, clearing the scene for just a moment.

There's a stone alter just a few feet from me. Stones stacked to support a giant slab. And surrounding it are smoldering logs, placed in a precise, exact circle. There are no flames, but I feel the heat rising from them, and I'm consumed in sweet smelling smoke. It billows in the air, thick and heady.

"Cyrus," I say, my brows furrowed as I watch him hustle around the circle of smoldering logs, carefully adding them here and there. "What are you doing?"

He doesn't even look over at me, just continues about his work. "We must hurry, *im yndmisht srtov*," he says. "We must prepare before the time has passed."

"What time?" I ask, tracking him with my eyes as he moves. "What are we preparing for?"

He places his last log, standing behind the alter, across the circle from me. "They only occur once every few centuries," he says. His eyes are hectic, frantic. He looks around, double-checking his strange work. "My parents…" He turns in a circle. He grabs a stick that was lying just outside of the circle and prods a log back into place. "My parents spoke of the power of the darkness during the light. Before they died, they lamented over and over, if only such a powerful celestial event was occurring…" He prods another log. "They would not have died."

I step forward, feeling desperately confused. "Cyrus, I don't understand. But we need to talk. So much…so much has happened."

Cyrus suddenly stills, and I nearly collide with him. He stands straight and his eyes snap to me.

My racing heart freezes as I stare into those eyes. I feel my entire body relax, go to a peaceful place where I know everything will be okay.

He raises a hand, tracing his fingertips down my cheek. "I know, my love," he says quiet and soft. "But I also know the greatness you are capable of."

I take a step closer, closing the distance between us. I look up into his eyes and feel the longing in me double.

We're so close, physically. But not near close enough.

"You are lost, my love," I say as I reach up and place my hand on his cheek. He presses his face into my hand, his eyes sliding closed for a moment. "Come back to me."

He opens his eyes again, but they rise up, rise up to the sky. "I am trying, my love," he says, still staring at the sky. And I realize, we have been standing out in the day, but slowly, the world is growing colder and darker. "I am searching for the way back. So we must prepare. You must be ready. It will be soon, when the day is dark as the night."

MY HEAD SNAPS UP AND I'M STARTLED WHEN MY surroundings are dim and the walls around me feel crushing and suffocating.

My neck is stiff. I look down to see the table my cheek was resting upon.

Sitting right above where my head rested is a body.

Cyrus.

I realize as I stand up that I worked myself into exhaustion. I fell asleep here in the lab.

I lean over, double-checking all the work I did last night. Cyrus skin is still smudged with black marks where I rubbed the ash over every bit of him.

Gently, with careful fingers, I touch his neck.

A gasp. A peaceful breath. They exist in the same moment when I see it.

Tissue. Soft and pink. Fragile and thin.

I see muscle reattaching. I see skin touching skin, knitted back together.

"Cyrus," I whisper as I place a hand against his cheek. "I knew you would find a way back."

But do I, really? Cyrus' body may be repairing itself, helped by my science and magic. But where is he? Where is his soul? His mind?

That wasn't a memory I just had. As I search back

through the thousands of years and lives, I know that scene was nowhere in history.

Was it just the desires of my imagination?

What it just my longing for my husband and answers to my desperation?

We must prepare.

Prepare for what?

Was Cyrus there, in my mind, reaching out for help?

"I don't understand," I say as I look down at his broken body. "What must I do?"

Cyrus does not answer me.

I turn, crossing to the fire pit and coat my hands in ash once more. I rub a fresh coat on Cyrus' face, run my hands down his arms. I coat his own hands. I spread it all over his body.

Next I fetch a bowl from the shelves. Squatting beside the grotto, I reach down far, digging my fingers into the pebbled sand and mud on the sloping edge. I collect herbs, dozens of centuries dried out. I wish I knew more, knew everything about their use and purpose. There are so many more here than there once were when we lived back in our home country and Cyrus used them to heal the sick and afflicted. But I take some of this and some of that, mixing it into my mud.

I return to Cyrus' side with strips of muslin I find on the shelves. I set them and the bowl beside his body.

Lastly, I take a knife and slice the blade of it across the palm of my left hand. Blood instantly wells. I make a fist, forcing the blood to flow and drip, and hold it over the bowl, letting it drip into the mud and herbs.

My blood. It turns the mixture dark and red.

I use my own hands to mix it all together. I blend it until it's smooth and consistent.

"Bring him back to me," I pray as I dip the strips of muslin in the mixture. I coat them until they are saturated. And then carefully so as not to disturb the healing tissue, I wrap the strips around Cyrus' neck. I wind them around, fully saturated with mud, and herbs, and the blood of the person who loves him most in this universe.

"Come back to me, *im yndmisht srtov*," I say quietly, over and over.

When I am finished, I stand with my hands braced on the table, my head hanging low.

I'm exhausted mentally.

I've run through this over and over and tried to understand my strange vision. I've tried to consider what his healing flesh means, the reality of what is possible.

"Please," I beg, putting everything into my words. "Give him back to me."

I take a breath as my head rises back up.

I feel the time that has passed since I came down here. I know each minute that has ticked by.

I've done everything I can for Cyrus. I've prayed all the prayers, used all the dirt magic I know.

All I can do now is wait. Try to understand what he was telling me in the dream.

Right now, I have an entire kingdom in upheaval. Right now, I need to go be the queen of all vampires.

"I will be back soon, my love," I say quietly as I bend. I

press my lips to Cyrus' forehead. I press my palm to his cheek, gently brushing my thumb over his skin.

And then I step away. I cross to the hidden door and walk out, leaving my husband to heal, hidden in the belly of the castle.

As it should be, it's absolutely silent when I step back into the hallway. Even with my enhanced hearing, I can't detect a single sound except the air moving through the hallways.

With determination, I head down the hall. I turn right at the end of it. I head up a spiral staircase. I cross another hall, pass a huge ballroom. I turn at a meeting room. I ascend another set of stairs.

There at the end of the hall, I see the doors.

Huge and ornate and black, they stand fifteen feet tall. There are scenes carved into the wood. The battle with our son. Two trees with roots that lead to dozens of others. Another tree sits at the top of the door, beneath a beautiful sky—the place where Cyrus and I married in my first life.

It tells the story of us.

I feel heavy as I walk down the hall toward it. So filled with time. So weighted by responsibility.

The doors easily swing open when I pull on them.

And I'm overwhelmed by the scent of Cyrus.

Time. Pine. Sandalwood.

I feel Cyrus in every corner of this room. And a million memories rush through me.

A huge bed sits in the center of the room. A black bedframe supports the big bed, a black comforter and pillows make it look inviting. A desk is pushed up against the window, currently covered with solid metal shutters. Pictures are hung on the walls, each of them showing a scene of Cyrus and I together. All of them are paintings. We have not been reunited since modern photography was invented.

And hanging above our bed is the black crystal chandelier.

Memories threaten to overtake me. So I take the opposite approach. I push them away. Every single one of them.

I turn to the bathroom, a room that was merely storage when we first made the castle our home, and has since been updated with modern conveniences. A massive shower with four showerheads awaits me.

I crank the water as hot as I can, and burn off the horrors of the past twenty-four hours.

Getting myself presentable is a challenge. While everything I've ever owned is here—brushes, mirrors, they are so dated they're hardly usable. I have not used them since I wore La'ei's face, and that was nearly three hundred years ago.

I make a mental note to send someone—once I know who I can trust—to get me modern things—hair dryers, curling wands, makeup.

For now, I wear a bare face and have to let my hair dry in the simple braid I tie over my shoulder.

The closet is bigger than the entire apartment I shared with Amelia back in Greendale.

I smile at one side, filled with Cyrus' clothing, most of it modern and sleek, but much of it incredibly old. I recognize which suit he wore to a certain grand ball and the ensemble he wore to preside over a specific execution.

The other side is filled with my clothing. All of it ancient. But it all looks dusted and fresh. It has been taken care of and updated, in preparation for my return.

And toward the back of the closet, I find what I am looking for.

Garment bags hang, fresh and modern.

I open them to find new clothes, all in my size. Leather and cotton and silk. Cyrus prepared for the moment I would return home to Roter Himmel.

I know the role I must play today. So, I dress the part.

I pull on black leather pants. I find a blood red blouse, sleeveless, but with a high collar. Black stitches and strategically placed buckles make it look fierce, while being practical for fighting, if necessary. I finish off the look with combat boots.

Lastly, I cross back into our bedroom. I go to the painting of Cyrus and I from the seventh century and swing it away from the wall. I press on the third stone down. Next, I cross to the lantern hanging from the wall and twist it forty-five degrees to the left.

I hear a latch release and walk to the ornate rug covering the floor at the foot of the bed. I slide it back, revealing the barely discernable door in the floor.

Lifting it, I drop down the stairs.

The space is not large. Maybe ten feet by ten feet. But the walls are lined with every kind of weapon imaginable. Stakes. Guns. Bombs even.

Only two people in the world know that there is a panel that lifts out of the back wall, opening to a passageway that leads down a tunnel that opens up into the water, an escape

from the castle right into the lake, over two miles away—
Cyrus and I built it as we waited for the war with our son to
begin, just in case we ever needed it.

There are so many places in the castle no one knows
about other than Cyrus and myself.

I arm myself with two stakes and a gun with glass bullets
—I've never seen anything like it, but I can just imagine
what it is capable of. I grab a wicked-looking knife too, just
for good measure.

Closing the weapons room, I lock our bedroom behind
me, and set back off through the castle.

The castle is roughly made up of six main levels. There
are other side branches, other tunnels leading to secret
destinations, like the lab, but generally, it equates to six
levels.

The main entry to the castle, where it lets out on town
level, is the third floor. It also houses the Grand Hall, the
library, and other high-use rooms. The majority of the quar-
ters are on the second floor, along with both our offices. Our
bedroom is on the upper-most first floor.

The fourth floor houses more ballrooms and a few quar-
ters. It also has the kitchens. The fifth floor is dingy and dark
and where the politicians hang out. The sixth floor, dark and
secluded, houses the prison, where I head now.

I don't hesitate as I cut my way toward the prison. I've
walked these halls and passageways thousands of times. I
cleared the debris from those rooms, scrubbed the soot from
those walls. I found bear cubs hiding in that hallway.

Down I descend into the dark, lighting torches as I go.
The air grows colder, damper. Thicker.

I descend the last set of stairs and grab a pair of sunshades from a shelf on my way inside.

Brilliant sunlight scatters throughout the space. There are twelve prison cells, each of them divided with a solid steel wall. Steel gates hold the prisoners captive. And in every one of the cells, there is a tube that rises up to the outside world. They are lined with mirrors, to reflect and intensify the sun.

My eyes scan the cells as I walk along. The first is empty. As is the second. There is a woman in the third; I can't tell if she's alive or not. She lies on her stomach on the stone floor, her hair covering her face, her hands cupped around it in an attempt to block out the sun. But she does not move, and I'm not sure she's even breathing.

The fourth cell is empty. And the fifth.

But in the sixth cell, I find the man I'm looking for.

I don't say anything, don't make any kind of sound to make my presence known, though surely he can still hear me. I watch him—observe.

He's a dirty man who seems to have resurrected around the age of thirty or so. Thin hair sits atop his head, balding before he got the stones to take his own life and stop the ageing process. He's lanky and soft looking. Very un-vampire like.

He sits huddled in the corner of the cell, his face tipped into the stones. He holds his hands over his eyes. His entire body trembles.

Weakling. He's only been in here a few hours in the sunlight.

I remember. Cyrus held Alivia and Ian here for over a month.

"How did you get into the castle?" I start with the least important question.

The man takes in a sudden breath, his shoulders, dropping. As if he truly didn't hear me enter the prison. Slowly, not fully removing his hands from his eyes, he turns. He peers at me with glowing red eyes. Venom fills them, but he still quakes. Even through the smile that grows on his face.

He turns, kneeling on the ground and starts crawling toward me on his hands and knees. He can barely keep himself upright, he shakes so hard from the pain of his fully, incredibly enhanced dilated eyes.

The man stops at the bars to the cell, crouching. His hair hangs into his face, but it does little to protect his eyes. Not only do his irises glow red, but the whites of his eyes have thick, violent red veins popping up in them.

"This is indeed a fascinating time in our history," he says. His voice is surprisingly deep. It rumbles in his chest and reverberates against the stone walls. "For centuries we have seen the King lead without his Queen. But never, in all these years, have we seen how the Queen leads on her own."

I feel very calm inside, and very cold. I'm made of stone, utterly quiet and controlled and strong.

"Something in me tells me you are not a Royal," I say, staring at him. Nothing about him indicates he is any kind of a Royal. Not his demeanor, nor his body, nor the smell rolling off of him. "Everyone in our world knows only Royals are permitted within the borders of Roter Himmel. So how did you get in?"

The man laughs, wrapping his dingy hands around the

bars. "In times of peace, minds are at ease and suspicions are down. Borders are patrolled with easy eyes."

He snuck into the city. Not that difficult to do, really. There are endless mountains that surround us. There are a hundred different ways you could slip into the city without The Guard knowing.

But the fact that he got through the city, into the castle without a Royal detecting him and sounding the alarm, that is what worries me.

He should have been caught. Someone should have detected him. Someone should have said something.

"I'm going to ask you some more specific, harder questions," I say as I reach into the sleeve sewn into my pants. I remove the knife. "I know your instinct will be to be vague, to not directly answer my questions, to laugh and smile like a knowing little cockroach." I bring the blade up, staring down its polished surface. "But this is your one warning. I do not have much time for games. I don't like performing interrogations. So be direct, and I'll be merciful on your body."

There. That is what I want. That little falter in his gaze. The slackening of his disgusting smile.

He tries to hold the façade, but I see it slip.

And I smile.

"How many of you are there in this plot to kill Cyrus and change the monarchy?" I ask, looking him dead in the eyes.

He looks at my blade, as if deciding just how much it will hurt when I use it on him. He smiles again, looking up at me with his red eyes, smiling. "Just me."

I turn away from him, walking to the cupboard against

the stone wall. Swinging the doors open, I reach inside and grab one of the circular orbs resting on the shelf.

I spin, and toss it into the cell, where it lands on the floor just to the side of the man. It shatters, and a small cloud of gas envelops him.

He shouts, coughing. He attempts to scramble away from it, but his limbs keep giving out on him and he falls half on his side, half on his face.

I grip the chair sitting in the corner. I drag it across the stone floor. The gate screeches loudly as I unlock it and swing it open. The man moans and whimpers on the floor as I walk into the center of the cell and set the chair upright.

He twitches, as if he thinks he can make a run for it, but his muscles have been frozen, and pain rockets through his body, rendering him unable to do anything but speak and process pain.

I grab him by the front of his disgusting shirt and haul him up. He nearly falls out of it when I throw him into the chair. His head lolls from one side to the other, resting at a downward angle to the left.

"I did warn you," I say as I stand before him.

His face contorts in pain as his nerves are pummeled.

"I tried to be level and easy to work with," I say as once again I hold the knife at my side. "Perhaps you did not take me seriously because I am a woman. Because I am the Queen, and not Cyrus. But today is a day to learn, I suppose."

I walk forward. I raise the knife, touching it to the tip of his chin. I still feel absolutely calm. Confident. Controlled. "Now tell me," I say quietly. "How many of you are there?"

"Within the city?" he says, his eyes flicking up to mine.

They're wide, flooded with fear. "Only five others, beside myself."

"And outside the city?" I prod further.

He gives a tiny shake of his head, which causes the tip of my blade to press further into his chin. He immediately stops. "It's a movement that has been growing for years, centuries."

"This isn't anything new," I say. "There's always been Born who have tried to take Cyrus off the throne. What makes this movement any different?"

His mouth slowly closes and his eyes drift up to mine again.

"I've heard rumors that some of the Royals are turning against us," I say. My voice is quiet. I lean in closer, leveling my eyes to his. "Are you working with them?"

His eyes grow hard and dark. "We had a choice to make. If we trusted them or not. How far do you trust members of the family who looked down upon you for so long? But in the end, what choice do we have, if we want things to change?"

I truly didn't think he'd have the control or strength.

But suddenly he lunges forward, his hand wrapping around my wrist. Smooth and quick, he yanks the blade forward, and buries it into his own heart.

"Say your goodbyes, Sevan," he says in a raspy voice as he slumps into the chair. "The change has already begun, your world will never look the same."

With horror coursing through my body, I let my hand fall, the knife clattering to the stone floor. And the man slumps, falls off the chair, and lands on the floor with a dead thud.

"Shit," I hiss as my hands fist into my hair. "No, no, no."

I need more information. I needed so much more information out of the one individual I know for sure is involved in this conspiracy.

I feel my eyes ignite. I know what must be done.

I turn, leaving the dead man on the floor, and stalk back up the stairs.

CHAPTER 3

THERE'S A RUCKUS ECHOING THROUGH THE CASTLE WHEN I
level onto the main floor. Shouts of anger and questions. As I
turn the corner for the main entry, I see Alivia standing there,
someone on their knees before her.

There's a crowd standing just outside the doors to the
castle. It's still evening, and the sun has not yet set on this
summer day, so every one of them wears a set of sunshades.

"The crown cannot treat us like this!" someone shouts.
"After all these years of loyalty, she treats us as if we are
traitors!"

"The king was beheaded!" Alivia shouts back. "There are
obviously traitors among you. What did you expect?"

"I've been a member of court for over three hundred years,
and never has the crown jumped to the conclusion of anarchy."

I step out of the shadows, and immediately, the crowd
shuts up. Wary eyes watch me walk forward, take note of

every move I make, of the set of my shoulders and the lift of my chin.

They each take half a step backward.

"She's right," I say, stopping in front of them. "I am thankful I was not here to witness it, but I know many of you saw it. When that man cut our King's head from his shoulders. When he murdered Cyrus. Roter Himmel is supposed to be a safe and peaceful place for us. Some are trying to change that, to ruin our entire world. So I beg of you, be patient while I sort out who it is we can trust."

I take note. Of those who look at me with understanding, of those who nod in agreement that we have to do everything we can to take down the betrayers. And I note those who look at me with disdain. Of those whose eyes are ignited red and whose lips are set in a thin, tight line.

"You," I say, pointing to a man with platinum blond hair and anger on his lips. "You," I move onto a woman whose fists are curled. "You." Another man. Another woman. One more man. All obviously upset with the way I am handling things. "Inside."

But they haven't entirely forgotten who I am. Their expressions falter. The look in their eyes goes from angry, to uncertain.

But they each step forward.

"Wait there," I say, pointing to the wall that leads to a passageway further into the castle. "Don't move."

They shuffle to where I tell them, but I don't watch them. I listen, straining my ears for sounds of movement and betrayal. But I turn my eyes to Alivia, who watches me with respect, and the man kneeling before her, with a blade pressed between his shoulder blades.

"He was attempting to leave?" I ask as I walk around to stand before him.

"He was," Alivia confirms. "I caught him trying to slip into the mountains, a bag over his shoulder." Her eyes slip up to mine. "Ian ran into two Born trying to leave as well. They're dead."

I nod, a sense of relief. The man in the prison told me there were five other Born in on this plot. Now there are only three left to worry about.

I look down at the man on his knees before us. He's a handsome man, young looking. Thick red hair covers his head, accompanied by a well-maintained beard. He looks up at me with piercing green eyes.

"Did you not receive word that the Queen commanded no one was to leave Roter Himmel?" I ask. Again, my voice is calm, even. Confident.

He doesn't say a word, only stares up at me with cold eyes.

"Give me your arm," I say.

He doesn't move until Alivia digs her knife into his back. His face winces in pain and he bows away from the blade. His eyes are angry and hard when he opens them again and looks back up at me.

He raises his arm.

My fangs lengthen and toxins pool in my mouth. I take his wrist, and raise it to my lips.

I bite into his flesh, and draw in his blood.

A taste is all I need. Just a second later, I release him.

Royal, a descendant of Dorian.

"Tell me," I say as I release his arm, blood dripping to the floor as his arm hangs at his side. I lick his blood from my lips. "Are you simply a coward, terrified of what was to come now that your King is dead? Or do you have more sinister motives? A message of success to deliver? Were you looking to betray your kind?"

"I am not a coward," he says. His accent is heavy, but I can't quite identify it. German. Irish. Something else. "But I do recognize that our world is about to change beyond recognition now that the King is dead."

We stare at one another. I wish I were better at reading people. I wish I could see it in his eyes if he is telling the truth or not. But he just stares at me blankly.

I want to have mercy. I want to just send him to the prison, to interrogate later. But I feel eyes on me, dozens of them. I feel their judgment. I can sense their doubt.

The Queen made a promise as to what would happen if anyone tried to leave Roter Himmel.

I have to set the example from the very beginning.

"Take him to the prison," I say. "We'll ship him off to the desert tonight."

"No," the man says, his eyes widening. Panic licks into every crease of his face. "You must forgive me! I *was* afraid."

I turn to leave, but look over my shoulder. I feel sick. Like a heavy, wet stone is slowly sliding down my throat before dropping into my stomach. "I warned you. *You* made this choice."

Alivia grabs him roughly by the back of the neck and drags him up to his feet. He tries to fight her, but she jabs a needle into his neck. He howls in pain, his steps faltering, before he falls flat on his face, moaning and crying in anger and pain.

"You remember where to take him?" I tentatively ask Alivia as she drags him over the floor.

"I'll never forget," she says without looking back up at me, or anyone else.

She makes her way down the passageway, dragging the man, until they are out of sight.

"I mean it when I tell you this: Do not leave," I say, turning back to the crowd outside. "We need to keep our kind safe, and the only way we can do that, is by figuring out who is trying to betray us. You'll be rewarded for your cooperation."

I'm grateful for those who nod in solemn promise. I'm grateful for those who bow, and mutter, "Yes, my Queen."

I turn back to those six I lined up against the wall. "Follow me," I say.

I know the danger I'm putting myself in as I lead them down the hall. As we descend these stairs, it would be so easy for them all to gang up on me and take me out. A quick stake through the heart, the quick snap and pull of my neck, my head would be gone, and I'd be dead—again.

But no one steps out of line as we step down to the fifth floor. We work our way through the dim corridor and then I turn into a room. A bench dominates the center of the room, and against the far wall, is a door.

I incline a hand toward the bench, indicating for them to take a seat. They seem wary, but each of them does.

"I'm not going to give a speech and try to convince you

I'm doing the right thing," I say, standing beside the door. "I don't owe any of you an explanation. You." I point to the woman on the end of the bench. "Come with me. The rest of you wait here if you value your immortal lives."

The woman gives a backward glance at the rest of the crowd, but she does stand, and tentatively follows me through the door and into the room.

It's a small room. Ten by ten. In the center there is a simple table and a chair on either side of it.

"Please sit," I tell her. I do not do so myself however.

She sits and I take her arm. "Considering how long it has been since I last was able to get to know the inhabitants of Roter Himmel, I can't rely on facial memory to identify the Royals," I begin to explain. "And since Cyrus is not at my side to assist me, I have to rely on the only test I can trust."

Her eyes widen for just a moment before I raise her arm to my lips and sink my fangs into her wrist.

Royal. A descendant of Dorian.

I immediately release her.

"Thank you for your cooperation," I say, though I'm pretty sure I sound disingenuous. I round the table and take a seat across from the woman. "What is your name?"

Her brows narrow and she wipes the blood on her wrist onto her pants. "Diana."

"And how long have you lived at Court, Diana?"

She leans forward, bracing her forearms against the edge of the table. Her features are hard, her face angular. I think she just permanently looks angry. "For about three hundred years."

"And you were born here, yes?" I prompt.

She nods.

I smile, nodding. "I would like to tell you a story, Diana," I say, mirroring her posture. "A story of when our kind very first came into being. When my husband made himself into the ultimate hunter, but also cursed himself with the craving of blood."

Diana's eyes widen a bit and her entire body tightens slightly.

"I watched in horror as he hunted down his first human. I saw his tears as they fell down his face in remorse. Cyrus, the first vampire, like yourself, craved blood and he could not resist the urge to drink. So people went missing and the rumors began to spread in our town."

I can picture it all. Every detail. Every memory. The beginnings when I wore the face of Sevan and had never died a single death.

But in this moment, I pay exact attention to my words. I control every line and every thought.

"And then when there were two of us, the whisperings grew louder. Dark eyes turned our direction. Our lives were torn apart. We had to leave, or we knew they would turn against us."

I shiver as I think of that first night in the forest.

"We lived like animals in the woods," I continue. "And every night, we moved, because always during the day, they hunted us through the forest. With knives and primitive weapons. We didn't know how they would hurt us. For months and months we were driven from place to place, constantly pushed by fear."

Diana sits there, very, very still. Frozen. She's hardly even breathing as she listens to my story.

"After I gave birth, we were once more on the run. One of us would always kill, and most of the time we were not discovered, but the times we were..." I shiver, remembering the terror. "We were strong, we could defend ourselves, but it was the two of us against the entire world. A population of billions."

I look up and meet her eyes. I lean forward slightly, our faces only a foot apart.

"Roter Himmel was a god-send," I say. "After years of living in fear and uncertainty, we had somewhere safe. Somewhere we did not have to hide what we were. We grew our family here. We loved and cherished here."

I sit back, my eyes darkening. "There are over eight billion people in this world, Diana," I say straight and blunt. "There are roughly fifty-thousand vampires, Born, Royal, or the few Bitten left, throughout the world. There are forces at work in this moment that are trying to destroy Roter Himmel. They would expose our kind to the world, perhaps to change the system. To create a new monarchy. Perhaps to attempt to take over the world."

I sit forward again, locking my eyes on hers. "Fifty-thousand of us, eight billion of them. I'm not willing to take on those odds and lose the peace and protection of Roter Himmel. Are you willing to take that risk, Diana?"

Her expression has been going slack, slowly, over this entire story time. Her eyes are open, her lips slightly parted.

"We all look the same, loyal or betrayer," I say. "This may take some time. But if even one of them slips through the cracks, it could mean the end of us all. Are you ready to take the risk, Diana?"

She blinks five times, as if clearing the fog of my story from her brain. "No," she whispers.

"Do you want to be hunted one day, 160,000 to one?" I ask her.

"No," she immediately says.

"Do you understand why I must be careful and thorough?"

"Yes, my Queen." She says it with a little bow of her head.

"Do you swear fealty to the crown, and to protect Roter Himmel and everything it stands for?"

She meets my eyes, and the change is astounding. She rises to her feet and then kneels before me. "I swear it, my Queen."

A small smile forms on my lips. I take her hand in mine, and pull her to her feet as I stand. "Then go. Bring them into the castle. One by one. Test their blood for Royalty. Tell them the story I have told you. And rely on your instinct to know if they can be trusted and believed when they swear allegiance to our kind."

"Yes, my Queen," she says once more.

I cross to the door with her. Her face is pale white when she looks back at me just once, and I understand: it's a terrifying possibility of what could happen if we are not careful.

The others watch her closely as she walks past them, and then their eyes jump to me.

"You," I say, pointing at the man on the end of the bench.

IT TAKES TWO HOURS, BUT ONE BY ONE, I TEST EACH OF their blood. They're all Royal, as I was quite confident they would be, but not entirely certain considering the circumstances. One by one, I tell them the story of the early days of running, fearful for our lives. I add more and more detail with each retelling. By the time I finish the story with the last woman, she is tearful and trembling.

I lay out the numbers for them. Explain how few of us there are, how we are just little specks in this gigantic world.

I watch them closely as we speak. I rely on my gut, search deep down for the answer to the question: will this person betray me?

But I see it in their eyes—they may not have been happy with me just hours ago, but they understand now.

One by one, I send each of them out of the room to assist in the interrogation of the four hundred residents of Roter Himmel.

What they do not know is that this is not enough for me. Words are only words, they mean so little.

I'm going to need proven proof of loyalty.

CHAPTER 4

I'M SO DAMN EXHAUSTED.

For ten minutes, that's all I dare take, I sit in that interrogation room by myself, just staring at a wall. For ten minutes, I let it all wash over me, let it overwhelm me. Everything I have to do. Everything I'm dealing with.

And when my ten minutes are up, I stand, hold my chin high, and I walk out of the room and down the hallway toward the stairs. Through passageways and down through the belly of the castle and mountain into our secret tunnels.

My heart pounds when I stand outside of the lab.

What if?

What if?

What if?

Emotion makes my throat tight. I have to rein in my imagination from getting too dark, but also too hopeful.

"Face reality, woman," I quietly say to myself. My voice reverberates madly off the stone walls, a chorus of reminders.

I open the hidden door and step into the lab.

The torch still glows dimly against the far wall. Shadows dart wildly as my movements send the flames dancing for a moment. The air is warm, humid. It's comforting.

My eyes dart straight to the table, and on it, Cyrus still lies. I swallow once as I cross the space to him, my mouth feeling dry.

"Hello, my love," I say as my voice threatens to crack.

He still lies there, utterly still, not breathing.

But as I remove the bandages and look closer at his neck, hope floods through me.

More tissue has reconnected. Barely still visible, I see white bone reattached. I see nearly whole muscles. His skin is slowly knitting back together.

Cyrus' body may heal. But will he actually return to me?

Will I get Cyrus back? Or will I only end up with a husk? A body that looks like my husband, but isn't?

"I know you are lost right now," I say quietly as I sit beside him, lying my head on the table, our faces only two inches apart. "That you're so confused and thrown into chaos. But I'm here, Cyrus." I reach up, taking his hand in mine, lacing our fingers together. "I've been in the darkness, too. But in the end, we always find our way back to one another. Keep searching for me, Cyrus."

I bring his hand to my face and gently press my lips into his skin.

"I'm right here, Cyrus," I say softly.

I feel myself grow heavy.

I'm so tired.

So exhausted.

So overwhelmed.

So when it calls, I let sleep pull me down into its depths, hoping and praying that I can find my forever heart again.

A SLIVER OF LIGHT SEARS MY EYES. MY HAND DARTS UP, adjusting the sunshades on my face, once more safely blocking out the sun.

My head tilts, grass rustling beneath me.

And there, lying beside me, is my husband.

"Cyrus," I breathe with a smile.

He lies in the grass beside me, a pair of sunshades on his own face.

We lay in a field, beneath the brilliant sun. Just the two of us.

"*Im yndmisht srtov*," he says gently as a little smile grows on his lips.

I roll over and Cyrus tucks me into his side. I rest my head on his chest, taking in a deep breath. Peace washes through me.

There's nothing, nowhere in the world either of us needs to be. Nothing to take care of. Just Cyrus, just me. Here. Together.

"I found you," I say, resting my hand on his chest. His comes up to mine, cupping it tightly.

"Not yet my love," he says and I feel his eyes rise. "The time is nearly here. We must be prepared."

"Prepared for what?" I ask, looking up at his face.

"You will only have minutes," he says, his eyes still fixed on the sky.

"Cyrus, I-"
But the world grows dark. The temperature drops.
And I feel him slip away.
All there is, is air.

CHAPTER 5

I STARTLE AWAKE, JERKING UP IN MY CHAIR. IN CONFUSION, I look around, expecting tall grass and blinding sun.

But it's comfortably dark. And I'm surrounded by stone.

I look at Cyrus, see his beautiful face. But he doesn't open his eyes. His lips do not twitch with the prospect of words. He lies there perfectly still. Perfectly dead.

I've already lost too much time, and I have no idea how much of it has passed. Jumping to my feet, I restock the fire, burning two small logs. I get new bandages, gather fresh mud from the grotto. In a bowl, I mix the ashes, the mud, some herbs, and my own blood.

The bandages immediately soak through when I dip them. Carefully, so I don't disturb the healing tissue, I wrap Cyrus' neck once more. I get down on my knees beside the table he rests on, and I offer up a prayer to anyone who might hear me, begging for him to be returned to me.

And even though it's the hardest thing I've ever had to

do, I walk out of that lab, having to trust and hope. Because I am the Queen, and our people need a leader.

Up and through the castle I rise. Up through the fifth floor, and then the fourth. And then on the main floor, just as I round the stairs, I nearly run straight into Eshan.

"E," I breathe, immediately pulling him into my arms. It's incredible, we have only been in Roter Himmel for two days, and already so much has happened. I miss my brother. "Are you okay?"

"Yeah, I'm fine," he says, his voice sounding a little panicked, despite what he just claimed. "Where the hell have you been, Logan? There's been some serious, heavy stuff going on, and no one knows where you've been!"

My eyes darken as my brother lets go of me and glares at me. "What's happened?" I demand as I start walking, even though I don't really know where I'm most needed at the moment.

"Those people you told to do the interviews," he says, walking beside me, much faster than I can on his long legs. "They're done. They've interviewed everyone in the…kingdom." He hesitates, says the word a little tight. Because I get it. For me this is normal, what I've done for centuries. But this is all brand new for him. It's all like something from a TV show. "They sent five people to the dungeon, or prison, or whatever."

"Good," I say, feeling hopeful. Like maybe we'll actually get a resolution to this problem.

"I'm not done," he says.

Down the hall, I hear a rumble of voices. They grow with each step. They come from the great hall.

"*Everyone* from this place, they're all here," Eshan says, slowing as we turn, the doors to the great hall coming into view.

There, stepping through, Alivia walks toward me.

She's dressed in sophisticated-looking clothes. Black and white and regal. Her hair is done up in a serious but elegant bun.

Her expression is grim.

And in her hands, she carries something golden and shiny.

My crown.

My heart does a little sputter at the sight of it. The gold surface, polished and hardly worn down. The glittering diamonds. The gleaming rubies.

Alivia—my mother, and the leader of the House of Conrath, stops just in front of me. There's worry in her eyes, but also belief.

"How bad is it?" I ask, my gaze flicking to the great hall. I see dozens of bodies standing inside. I don't recognize anyone.

Not everyone survives centuries and millennia.

"They just want answers," Alivia says. "They're scared and they don't know what to expect."

I see someone shift at the doors and find Ian and Mina there, watching me, but also, I get the feeling they're standing as a barrier. Between me…and them.

For just a second, I'm terrified.

I'm just a girl. I'm twenty-freaking-years old. I have the worst luck in the world. I lose everything. Even Cyrus now. I can't go in there, with all those vampires who have hundreds of years of experience in Court.

But as my eyes fall to the crown, I know what I have to do.

I've never been the one to lead. I never wanted to. Cyrus may have been brutal, but he was a man our kind could follow.

But I helped start this. I am the mother of them all.

I have to take on the crown.

With a tiny nod, I take it from Alivia's hands. Like a glove, it slides on my head, and I hold it high as I walk forward, flanked by a House leader, and my all-too-human brother, and step into the huge space, filled with my descendants.

I don't stop and greet any of them. I roll my shoulders back, pretending I am not wearing the same clothes I wore yesterday to torture a man, to conduct those interrogations, to sleep in the lab. I hold my chin up, perfectly balancing the crown on top of my head.

There they are. Two thrones. One for me, nearly always unoccupied. And the one for Cyrus. Carved out of the darkest African blackwood, they gleam, polished to the sheen of a mirror. Deep, rich red upholstery covers the seat and back.

Walking straight to the platform they sit upon, I stand in front of Cyrus' throne, and turn.

Four hundred sets of eyes stare back at me, waiting.

Tiny flickers of recognition jump out at me here and there. I remember that man, Dominic. And that woman, Pricilla. And those twins, Camilla and Cambrius.

That man there, he has to be Hector Valdez' son, Horatio.

But largely, I do not recognize the faces.

Eshan stands off to the side of the platform, joined by Alivia and Ian. Mina and Fredrick go to stand on my other side.

"I know you all know who I am," I say. And I'm surprised with myself. While I held such calm and confidence just moments ago, here, up on the stage, with every one of them looking at me, I'm overwhelmed and nervous. "I am Sevan. I've been gone for 286 years. Before that I was La'ei. And Jafari. And Antoinette. And now I am Logan Pierce. I grew up in the United States. I did not know what I was until Cyrus was called and then I died and remembered everything."

Every one of them watches me, expectantly, holding onto every single word I say.

"I know I look different, but I promise, I am her, the woman who married a man I loved. A woman who conceived, and gave birth to the one we all came to fear, the man called the Blood Father."

The mood in the room darkens just at his title. I'm fairly sure none of them were there, at the battle. They don't remember the seven years of war and darkness. But they all know the stories, back and front, the legends of the man who wanted to take over the world.

"I am the woman each of you stemmed from, can trace your lineage back to," I say. I have to swallow once, over-whelmed by that fact. But it does something to me. It warms my chest. It makes me look at them just a little differently.

Yes, thousands of years ago, every one of their bloodlines trace back to Sevan and Cyrus. But looking at them, after those thousands of years with new DNA, contributed to throughout the world, they all look so different.

But they are mine.

These people here: they are my family.

"But the King," a woman says. Her voice is breathy. Emotion pushes its way through. "What about Cyrus?"

I hate it. The fact that he lay there on display, alone and vulnerable for fourteen hours before I made it to his side to protect him. All of Roter Himmel saw how exposed, how defeated he was in that moment.

"The man who did that to him has been dealt with," I say through a tight throat. "I know for a fact there are three others who were in on the plot, and I swear, I will deal with them severely."

I try to read their faces, to pick out any other betrayers. But I just see their fear, their doubt.

"Is this the end?" a man asks. His tone tells me he doesn't want to ask the question, but he can't keep it in. "Now that Cyrus is dead, is this the end of Roter Himmel? Is this the end of peace?"

"Nothing will change," I speak up immediately. "Court will be chaotic and stressful in the weeks to come. But I swear, the Houses will continue to manage the world. Our existence and our safety will always remain our greatest priority."

"And who is going to enforce that?" a voice from the middle of the room pipes up. My eyes scan the room. An older man, older than the vast majority of those here at Court, with a wrinkled forehead and purplish lips is the one who spoke up. "You feel prepared to step up, and fill the role Cyrus has dominated for over two thousand years?"

I don't know if the crowd realized. How Ian slipped among them the moment the man finished his first sentence and began carefully making his way through the crowd. But I see it when he stands behind the man, and I have no doubt that he has a stake hidden, ready to use.

"No one," I vow very low and dangerously. "No one cares about preserving Roter Himmel more than I do." Emotion kinks my voice, and I hate it when it does.

But I see a light rise in the eyes of so many before me. Their sympathy and belief in me sparks.

"This is my home," I say. "I have lived dozens of other places, but at the core of every one of those lives, *this* is my home. And you are my people. My family. And I swear—I may do things differently than my husband ever did—but I *swear*, I will protect our home. Our people. Our kind."

"And when you starve," the ugly man pipes up again. "When you wither, and when you die, what is to become of us then?"

I've been putting on a show. Stalling. Putting on the bravado and leading for the time I must. Because I have to believe, with everything in me, that Cyrus will wake up. That this little known part of his curse will remain true. That he truly cannot be killed and he will wake up when his body has finished healing.

I believe Cyrus will awaken.

But none of them know that. None of them have reason to believe this isn't the reality.

So they've caught me here.

48

Because sure as time will continue to march on, at some point it will happen again.

I will starve. I will wither. And I will die.

"What then, Queen Sevan?" the man questions again with a dark look in his eyes.

Just then, the crowd gasps and steps away from him. He makes a choked off sound followed by a wet ripping sound.

Two figures stand beside the man, one holding a bloody heart in his hand. Their dark eyes glare out into the crowd, daring anyone to come against them.

I have never seen these men before with these eyes, but I know exactly who they are.

These are my grandsons.

Dorian and Malachi.

"What happens then is none of your concern," Malachi says, dropping the man's heart from his hand, letting it hit the floor with a wet smack.

"You may be members of court," Dorian says, his voice smooth, but utterly dangerous. "But it has never, ever been your place to question the All Mother."

Goosebumps flash over my skin and my heart races. Emotion pricks at my eyes.

"I've given you all my promises," I say. My voice is not as strong as I would like, but it carries clear and loud. "Be watchful. If we want to preserve our way of life, we must all watch for traitors. Because I have heard whispers that there are those of us here who want things to change. Be careful who you trust."

They look among themselves, like they can read the word off of each other's foreheads—*traitor*.

"You've been given all the answers you need," Malachi says. "Now get out."

They don't hesitate. One by one, they turn and slowly file out of the Great Hall.

And I bristle. With everything in me, heat and anger and bile rise, racing with the speed of flames.

Logan can't believe it. That they questioned *me*, that they did not clear out until a *man* told them to do so.

Screw them all, I think. *Things will change.*

Dorian and Malachi wait for the crowd to clear, watching each of them with darkness, daring them to challenge the commands. But they all leave, emptying the hall.

Emotion bites at my eyes when they both look at me at the same time.

Over thousands of years, these two, they have always been there, unwavering in their loyalty.

I take a step forward at the same time they step toward me. We meet in the center of the ballroom and I wrap an arm around each of their necks, hugging them in tight to me.

"Sevan," Malachi says with reverence. "You have finally found your way back to us."

"We are here, All Mother," Dorian says, hugging me tightly.

Slowly, the others behind me cross the space and with two tears slipping down my face, I let my grandsons go.

"Alivia," I say, turning to her. "This is Malachi, and Dorian."

She offers an empty little smile. "We've met."

Oh. Right.

Her trial.

"And Ian, I suppose you have, too?" I question.

He only gives a thin-lipped nod.

"Well then," I say, turning in Eshan's direction. "Dorian, Malachi, this is my brother, Eshan Pierce."

He looks terrified. But to my little brother's credit, he steps forward, and shakes Malachi's hand first, and then Dorian's.

"They're…" he stumbles over his words.

"Technically, they're my grandsons," I say, appreciating how weird this whole situation is for the Logan side of me. "But, considering this body never pushed any babies out, let's just leave it vague and call them family?"

We both huff out a little laugh that sounds the same. We might not share a speck of the same DNA, but being raised in the same house for thirteen years leaves a mark of similarity.

"It's a pleasure to meet you," Dorian offers with a warm smile and a little bow. He always was the one who could take a person in and make them feel comfortable, even in the middle of a horrific situation.

"How bad is it?" Malachi asks, getting right to the point. "Where is the King now?"

"He's safe," I say, slipping back into the reality of the present. "I've…there've been several attempts, stakes and sun torture. But never anything like this."

"It's true?" Dorian asks. He's already cringing. "Cyrus was beheaded?"

I press my lips into a thin line. I nod.

Malachi's eyes rise to Alivia's, and then to Ian's. "You trust them?"

I look over my shoulder at the both of them. While this is

still so new, so fresh, and hasn't exactly gone smooth so far, I know it. "I do. You can speak freely in front of them."

There's one more beat, and it's obvious: my family doesn't trust easily and they've seen no proof themselves.

"You already know that I know," Alivia cuts in, her voice sounding slightly annoyed. "I watched Cyrus get staked, right in front of me. I thought he was dead. And then watched him pull that stake out like it was just a little poke with a needle. I know that in the past, Cyrus really couldn't be killed."

They continue looking at her doubtfully.

"She went on trial for it, damn it," Ian growls. "We were both here. It's been all this time and Liv hasn't used that knowledge for a damn thing, so give her a break and respect her as a House leader, just like your pompous selves."

Malachi's eyes light to red and he takes one step forward.

Alivia throws a hand out, blocking her husband, at the same time I block Malachi.

"He's right," I say, pushing him back. "You may have different experiences, be closer related, but he's right." Malachi's eyes flick to mine in annoyance. "Alivia is the leader of a House, just like you and Dorian. I'm telling you that you can trust her, and you're going to listen."

Malachi is the leader of the House in Egypt. Dorian rules all of Russia with multiple Houses.

"I've seen Cyrus staked twice," I say, forcing a productive direction back into this conversation. "I've seen his body thrown off a cliff and shattered on the rocks below once. All times he should have died, all times he survived."

Dorian nods. "I was with him when he was nearly cut in

half by the Blood Father. He was down for a day while healing, but he did heal."

Malachi nods. "I was not standing beside him, but he was
stabbed through the heart more than once with a sword
during the years of war following the death of the Blood
Father."

"He always healed within a day or less, right?" I question, looking to each of them for confirmation.

They all concur.

"It's been three days now," I say. "He is healing, but there
are no signs of him waking up yet."

I feel cold.

I'm scared.

I want to hope, but I hardly dare.

"May we see him?"

All the blood drops into my feet when Dorian speaks
the words.

I look up at them with wide eyes. I turn them to everyone
who surrounds me.

This...this is the true trial of trust. Right now Cyrus is
safe. Right now I can protect him. I can defend his weakness
by not letting another soul see him like this.

But this is family. The people who have been the most
loyal to Cyrus for thousands of years are standing right here.

I nod. "Meet me in the infirmary in thirty minutes."

Without another word, I stride off, ducking out the doors.

CHAPTER 6

EVERY SECOND SINCE I'VE COME TO ROTER HIMMEL, I'VE been scared. Now is no different as I have to move Cyrus. I'm so careful, go so slow, so I do not disturb the healing tissues. But little by little, I move him. On silent feet, I rise up through the castle, transferring him to a gurney I brought from the infirmary. I wheel him through the empty castle.

After I wheel him into a secure room, I once more assess his healing.

I can't see bone any longer. Shiny muscle is barely still visible beneath his skin, but what little I can see is reattached. And most of his skin has knitted back together.

I expect that by morning, he will look normal once more.

I turn toward the door to wait for Dorian and Malachi, but I jump, a little yelp strangled in my throat when I find a body standing just inside the doorway.

"Larkin," I breathe.

There are many reasons why I trust him to do the things I ask, and his absolutely silent feet are two of the little ones.

"Everything has been taken care of back in the States, my Queen," he says, dipping in a small bow.

I can't handle any more emotion. This is something I need to process later, what Larkin had to do to cover up what happened to my parents. But I just don't have room in me for it right now.

"Thank you," I say, swallowing around my tight and thick throat. I look around, as if I can find and organize my thoughts from the air around me. There are too many strings I need to hold onto right now, and I'm pretty sure I'm dropping a lot of them.

"Things are a mess here," I say, looking back at the man. "I don't trust more than a few people. There are plots happening right under my nose. I don't have enough help or time to deal with it all."

"Give me an assignment," he requests simply.

I straighten, gratitude rushing through me.

Larkin has never been an official member of Court. He spends his own time moving from House to House, never staying in one place for long. But he's always here, whenever I'm alive, ready to serve.

Because I spared his life once. A long, long time ago, when I wore Helda's face.

"I've been told there were five other Born in Roter Himmel who were in on this plot to kill Cyrus," I say with a swallow. Larkin's eyes briefly flick to Cyrus, who lies behind me. "Ian Ward killed two already, but I don't know if the other three are still in the city or not. I need you to find them and get every drop of information you can out of them."

"It will be done, Sevan," Larkin says. He offers a deep bow, and immediately turns to leave.

I have all of ten seconds alone before there is the sound of footsteps down the hall.

I want to cover Cyrus up, to hide him. I can hardly bear the thought of Dorian and Malachi seeing Cyrus like this. But when I worked in the mortuary, we covered the dead with white sheets, and I've sworn to myself that I won't let Cyrus stay dead.

Their faces are already pale when Dorian and Malachi step into the room. When they see him, both of them swallow once, their faces growing even whiter. Slowly, they cross the room and stand beside him.

He looks better. Cyrus no longer just looks dead. He looks as if he could be sleeping.

"It hardly looks as if he was injured at all," Dorian says in awe. "And he truly was decapitated?" He looks over his shoulder at me.

My throat is thick when I nod. "I had to carry him, to move him out of the Great Hall," I say. "The King was in two completely separate pieces. Trust me."

I want to throw up at the memory of having to pick him up and arrange him like that.

"Incredible," Malachi muses. "How? How is this happening?"

"It's Cyrus' curse," I say. My eyes go glazed and I'm not really seeing anything anymore. "That he can never die, while I die over and over. The curse lives on."

They both shake their heads in wonder.

"Before all of this," I continue, waving my hand around the space, "Cyrus studied life. His parents were what you might call root doctors and astrologists. They taught Cyrus everything they knew. He claimed he didn't believe in it. But he used it. I watched him over the years. I was never an actual student, but I learned. I knew."

They watch me, but I don't look up.

"Ash for renewal," I say quietly. "Mud for grounding. Blood for life."

Someone kneels beside me, and it takes me a moment to find the will to bring myself back into the room. I blink, and let my eyes slide over to meet Malachi's.

"If anyone in the world can bring the King back from wherever he is, it is you, Sevan," he says. He reaches out and takes my hands in his.

I'm touched by his words and his display of compassion. Malachi has never been a warm or caring person. He has believed in alliances and power. Not in the way my son ever did. But in a way that made his lines strong, both physically and politically.

"Thank you," I whisper.

"We will protect the King," Dorian says. "If what you said is true and there are Royals looking to change things, we need a way to vet the entire Court, and maybe even beyond Court."

Malachi nods, and I know. Whatever has to be done, they're here to help me.

I feel something in me darken and harden.

"I think it's time to take a page out of my husband's playbook," I say as I stand. "I think we settle this with a game of sorts."

They look at me with surprise and uncertainty.

They have plenty of experience with Cyrus' games. But in all these thousands of years, I have never taken part, never condoned any of them.

"I have to believe Cyrus will return," I say as I stand tall. "I will not let it be to a Court—a Kingdom he cannot trust."

CHAPTER 7

EARLY IN THE MORNING, AN HOUR BEFORE THE SUN WILL rise, I make my way to the tower, where I sent word, via Dorian, for the others to wait for me. I wind my way up a spire, and when I reach the top, it opens up into a large room.

Arched windows wrap around the entire space. A golden chandelier with crystals dangling from it hangs from the high ceiling. A huge rug spans out across the floor. And comfortable chairs and couches and pillows are scattered around along the walls.

I find Eshan, Alivia, and Ian on the far side of the circular room, not really saying anything, just waiting.

A big huff whooshes out of my lungs when I sit down and let myself sink deep into the chair. My eyes immediately slip closed.

I'm not sleepy, but I'm exhausted.

I have an entire Court to keep in line, and about a dozen people I think I can trust to help me do it.

And suddenly, I realize I haven't fed in days.

"You're handling this all way better than I ever could have," Alivia says, attempting to lighten the mood.

I open my eyes, sighing as I stare at the ceiling. I'm too tired to even have a conversation, but I know it's needed.

"It will be easier now that Dorian and Malachi are here," I say. "This happens every time, to some degree. The Court doubts me because I look different, and it's been a really long time this time that I've been gone. But they respect and trust the two of them. It will be easier and quicker to get this figured out with them here."

I feel Alivia's mood darken. "Well, that's a load of bull shit."

I actually chuckle. "Amen." I sigh again, shaking my head. "Things change slowly in a place like this. We're all so stuck in time and that's the reality of it—they've never been led by anyone besides Cyrus."

"I just feel sorry for the idiots," Eshan pipes up. "Cyrus is pretty intense, but I grew up with Logan. She's damn scary!"

Everyone chuckles. But immediately I'm reminded that I should be chiding him for swearing.

It finally, suddenly hits me.

My parents are dead. Eshan is my charge now, for forever.

Emotion bites at my eyes. My throat clenches shut.

I bite my lower lip to try to keep from letting out a sob.

"Hey," Eshan says, climbing out of his seat and coming to my side. He wraps his arms around my shoulders and I immediately lay my head on his chest. "I'm sorry, Lo. I wasn't trying to be a jerk."

I shake my head. "It's not you." My voice breaks, but the tears don't fall yet. "I just remembered. It all just hit me that Mom and Dad..."

Eshan tightens his grip on me and I feel a tremble creep into his embrace.

I'd forgotten for a little while. With everything else, with Sevan so present in my head, I'd forgotten.

I'm still Logan Pierce. I'm still a twenty-year-old whose parents were just savagely murdered. I'm just a girl who now has to be in charge of her sixteen-year-old brother.

All while trying to hold a Kingdom together.

A sob rips from my chest and I hug into my brother tighter. A moment later, I feel a tear fall from Eshan's face and land on my ear. He cries silently, but holds me tight, keeping me together when it should be my job to comfort him.

But I can't right now.

Mom. Who taught me how to do my makeup when I was eleven. Who was so excited to go with me to buy my first training bra. Who loved to gossip about all the boys I liked in middle school.

And Dad. Who never remembered to buy anything new for himself, because he was always spoiling Mom rotten. Who snuck me out when I was fourteen to teach me how to drive. Dad was always up for going out for piping hot Buffalo wings every other Saturday for lunch.

Because of me, because of something I was born into and had no choice in, they're dead. They were brutally murdered by two men who have been hunting me for over one hundred years.

Alivia shifts to the chair next to me. She doesn't say anything and doesn't touch me. This is a world she can't be a part of. She may have given birth to me twenty years ago, but she wasn't there for any of those little moments. She doesn't know anything about the bond between my brother and I, and our parents that we looked nothing like.

But she's there. Just her presence screams her support.

I wipe my eyes after a while. I take a deep breath and straighten as Eshan releases me.

"We need to do it soon," I say. "If we wait any longer the bodies will be…" I can't say the words, but my training knows exactly the damage that has already been done to their bodies, and the state they're slipping further and further into without being taken care of. "Will you both help me?" I ask, looking to Alivia and Ian. "We need to lay them to rest."

"Of course," Alivia says as she takes my hand.

Without further words, we make our way down and through the castle. Alivia seems to know where she is going as she leads us toward the side entrance that lets out into the courtyard.

She opens a door just off to the side. Sitting just inside, in the center of the room, there are already two caskets.

I know. I already know that opening those caskets to see my parents' faces one last time to say goodbye wouldn't do one bit of good with the state they will be in. So, side-by-side, Eshan and I step inside.

I place my hands on one coffin that reads Gemma Pierce on the top of it. "I love you," I whisper. Trading places with Eshan, I go to my father's coffin. Ethan Pierce. "I'm so sorry," I whisper. "I love you."

Tears slowly slip down my face, and my brother's. Together, all four of us, we first take my mother, and then my father, and carry them out into the courtyard. In one corner of it, there is a graveyard, where over the years, Cyrus and I have buried our closest family members.

The graves were already dug. I don't know who did all of this, if it was Alivia or Ian, or maybe even Mina. But I'm incredibly grateful.

I don't even speak words, and neither does Eshan. But they're there, in the air around us. In our hearts. A lifetime of love.

And at the castle grounds, half a world away from their home, my brother and I lay our parents to rest.

CHAPTER 8

Maybe it's how I'm dealing with my grief, but after we go inside, I head to my office and call for Mina. I tell her to bring me a feeder. Ten minutes later she returns, and I drink and drink, and I only let the woman go when Alivia steps in and tells me that it is enough.

I lick my lips as I watch the woman wobble out on shaking legs with Mina's help.

I harden as I look back at Ian and Alivia. They sit on the plush couch against the far wall. I sit on the edge of my mahogany desktop, surrounded by a collection of things from all of my previous lives.

It's been unused for nearly three hundred years, but it's been taken care of as if I had been here just last week.

Eshan headed to bed. His human body needs it a lot more than the rest of us immortals.

"You can stop looking at me with those sad eyes," I say, reaching for the tiny skull that sits on one corner of my desk.

"Yeah, I'm an emotional mess right now and there's a lot of shit going on inside of me, but I have a ton of crap to take care of, and not a lot of time to do it, so please, just stop with the pity."

"You don't have to be a bitch about it," Ian growls. "We're just trying to help."

"This is how you can help," I snap, glaring at him. "If you knew anything about me, you'd understand."

I regret the words the instant they're out of my mouth. I close my eyes, letting out a slow breath through my nostrils. "I'm sorry," I say. "My nasty words get the best of me every once in a while."

I open my eyes to meet Alivia's, and there's this little look in her eyes that says, *I think I know where you get that from.*

"You're nearly all the help I have right now, and I do appreciate it," I say, trying to make it better. "I just...I can't deal with all the emotions piled up on top of the...stuff I have to figure out and do."

"I get it," Alivia says. "Everything I went through when taking over the House of Conrath made me into a little bit of a monster. And it's nothing compared to everything you have to tackle. So if being nasty helps, be nasty."

She actually pulls a little smile out of me.

It seems we have more in common than just our looks.

"Okay," I say with a sigh, turning the little skull over in my hand without really realizing I'm playing with it. "Something just the two...three," I correct, my eyes flicking over to Ian's. It's going to be a long, long while until we get along. "Of us need to talk about." I take one beat, my eyes sliding back to my biological mother's. "My father."

I see Alivia actually recoil a little bit. She sits further back in her chair, her shoulders draw in a bit.

"Have you seen him here at Court?" I ask, point blank.

Ian looks over at Alivia and I can read a lot in his eyes. He's worried for her. About how she's handling all of this. But he also hates this. The fact that she had sex with a man who wasn't him, even if it was years before they ever met, and something so heavy came of all this. Something that came back to haunt her and throw her life into so much chaos years later.

Ian is an asshole to me, to a lot of people in the world, I'd expect. But he does love Alivia, and I can see, he'll do whatever he can to help and protect her.

"Yes," Alivia says. She releases her breath as if she's been holding it. She looks pale. "He was in the Great Hall when all the others gathered for the...questions. I knew it was him immediately."

I'm actually relieved. This is one thing at least that is simple, black and white.

"Good," I say with a nod. "Now, you said you were pretty sure he gave you a fake name when you met him."

Alivia nods.

"So that raises one red flag," I say, looking at the little skull. I think it's from a squirrel. "And the fact that he ran into you, it just doesn't seem like a coincidence, does it? One Royal and another?"

She shakes her head. "I've thought about it a lot over the years," Alivia says. "I really don't know how he could have known I was a Royal, unless he happened to be following my dad, Henry. Once he learned I was alive, my dad used to check in on me every once in a while. I guess he could have followed Henry and made some assumptions."

"I don't know what it would have mattered," Ian says, shaking his head. "What's the point of a Royal male getting a still-human Royal female pregnant? The end result would have been the same if he'd gotten just any regular human female pregnant."

"So you think it was a coincidence?" I ask Ian.

He nods. "If it had been intentional, and he really had sought Alivia out, I mean, he would have recognized Liv yesterday. She wasn't hiding. Wouldn't he have remembered her and stepped forward to say something?"

He has a point.

"I think it was just a random hook up," Ian says. "All the Royals admit it, there are some who just sleep their way across countries trying to create more offspring. To either add power to their House, or, well, to try and make you." He gestures to me.

It makes me sick. But it's true. Cyrus greatly rewarded the families I was born into. When I was Edith, it was my father's major goal in life: to produce the offspring that would one day wake up as the Queen.

"I don't know," Alivia says, shaking her head. "It's just… the odds of this happening randomly? They just have to be non-existent."

She looks up at me, and I don't know what to say. "I don't know," I admit, shaking my head. "Both arguments seem solid and logical. I think for now though, we have to treat this like he knew what he was doing. I don't want to approach him yet, neither of us know anything about the man. But I think we need to see if he remembers Alivia or not. We have to test it."

Ian nods. "It would give us some answers. If he plays dumb and doesn't seem to remember Alivia, we'll be able to tell. If he admits to it, we'll know it was a power play and I'm sure he'll be happy to claim responsibility for bringing you back into the world. It would give us some answers."

I nod. "It's a start. Alivia, we'll have you discreetly identify him and then I'll have Mina bring him in."

She nods and I know Mina could hear everything when the door opens, revealing her, waiting just outside. Alivia and Ian stand, joining the menacing looking woman.

"Make him sweat first," I tell Mina. "Let him imagine the worst and he'll confess the truth easier."

Mina nods and the three of them leave.

CHAPTER 9

"You're sure about this?" Dorian asks as he takes his phone from his pocket. There's wariness in his eyes. They question and hope I will take it back. "You know this will take time. That this won't be resolved quickly."

"I understand that," I say. "Just do it."

Dorian and Malachi look at one another, each just as nervous about my plan as the other. But they take out their phones, and they make some incredibly life-changing phone calls.

I called this a game. But there is very little that is entertaining in all of this. This is tactical. It's black and conniving. This will scare the hell out of the people.

But I know it will work.

I stare out the window as Dorian and Malachi plan with their connections. We speak in Cyrus' office. There's a view out the front, one that looks out over Roter Himmel.

It's an enchanting town. The castle sits above the city.

There are two main roads, one that leads down from the castle toward the lake. The other cuts to this side of the lake, then wraps around it where it heads to the mountain pass, and eventually leads to the tiny town that supports the airport we use.

Homes dot the landscape here. Some small cottages. Others, large sprawling mansions. There are shops and markets. I see people milling about down there, just like this is their normal life. They shop. They raise their families.

But this isn't a normal town, those aren't normal lives.

Down there, there are Royal vampires and humans. They live in harmony. These humans know our secrets and willingly let us feed off of them. They are taken care of, in exchange for protection and financial security.

There is no other place in the world like Roter Himmel.

The Royals here don't have glory, they don't have attention. They don't lead Houses. But they get comfort. They can be their true selves, they don't have to hide. It's not like the outside world, where Alivia and Ian, and Lexington Dawes have to keep the secret of what they are.

We live in the open here.

And if I don't do something to protect it, others will try to tear it apart.

"It is done, Queen Sevan," Dorian says as he comes to stand at my side. "They will all arrive over the next two days."

Malachi then comes to stand beside me. "My armies have agreed, as well. They will be here shortly."

"Good," I say coldly as I look at the home I love so much. And my heart hurts.

Because I know the hell I am about to unleash on my people.

IN THE COMFORT OF THE BELLY OF THE CASTLE, I PUSH THE door open and slip inside the lab. The air is cool and crisp with moisture. I light the torches, casting the space in a warm glow of flame.

I force my heart to be calm as I walk across the room. Cyrus lies there in silhouette. With shallow breaths, I silently walk to his side.

Carefully, I remove the bandages, tossing them into the fire pit.

With reverence in my breath, I dare to look at his neck.

Smooth, creamy skin stretches from his chin to his collarbones. Unbroken flesh wraps around his neck.

He's healed.

Everything looks natural, as perfect as it did weeks ago when I said goodbye to Cyrus back in Greendale.

"Where are you, Cyrus?" I whisper.

My heart hurts. I ache. I want to reach inside his soul and search for anything to grab onto, any sign he is there, and pull him back into the here and now.

"I don't know what else to do, Cyrus," I confess. I place a hand on his cheek, caressing his face. "I've done everything I've watched you do. I've used blood and ash and mud. I've prayed and begged. I've done my part."

My lower lip trembles and I feel weak. "Now you have to find your way back to me."

I climb up onto the table, and gently, I raise his right arm, wrapping it around my shoulders. I rest my head on his chest. I press my forehead into his cheek.

I've touched a lot of dead bodies over the last year. They're cold. They turn hard and stiff.

Cyrus isn't cold, but he isn't warm. He isn't stiff, but he's dead weight.

I don't know if he's dead. He certainly isn't in a coma. But his soul certainly isn't in him right now.

"Where are you, *im yndmisht srtov*?"

I'm desperate, so that makes it harder. But I've found him in sleep before, so I tell myself to sleep, to sink into the dark.

And because I don't need it so often, and I have so much lately, it takes me at least two hours, but eventually, I slip between the folds of reality.

I SEE HIM SITTING ON A ROCKY OUTCROP THAT JUTS OVER THE lake. Across the field I walk, watching him the entire time.

He sits with his knees tucked into his chest, his arms wrapped around them. His shoulders are tense, the line of his lips, tight. The stormy sky above is reflected in his eyes, dark and serious.

I reach the base of the rocks and begin the short climb. I pull myself onto the flat landing and take the two steps to his side, sitting beside him.

"What's wrong?" I ask.

If I surprised him with my arrival, he doesn't show it. He just continues staring out over the lake.

"I think I'm finally tired," he says. His voice is shaky, just a little bit. Unsure.

"Tired?" I ask, my brows furrowing.

He doesn't immediately explain. He just stares, reflective. "It's been so long. The same patterns over and over. And here I fight to do it all again. I fight so desperately to get out of this hell. And for what? To do the same things over and over."

His words make my heart trip.

I have never, ever heard Cyrus speak this way.

"A life as long as yours is bound to get a little monotonous," I say, struggling to find some wisdom. "But that's the good thing about being individuals. We choose our direction, every day."

Cyrus shakes his head. "It's been so long. I think I'm finally tired, Sevan. But still, it comes. The dark during the light."

LIKE I WAS SLAPPED, I JERK AWAKE. I RISE UP ON MY ELBOW, looking down at Cyrus.

"No," I say, scrambling to my knees. I grip his shoulders, shaking him. "Don't you dare give up on me." I'm frantic, my words coming out too fast. "This is not over, Cyrus. This is not how you go down. We can change things. Don't you dare leave me here."

Tears pool in my eyes as I think about that empty look in his eyes.

Hell. That's what Cyrus said he'd been in.

Lonely, empty hell.

"Wake up, damn it!" I yell, shaking his body roughly. "I

need you, Cyrus! I won't let you leave me!" I slap him across the face as one tear slips down my face.

He doesn't react.

I breathe in a big breath, shifting so that I kneel beside him. I cover his mouth with mine and breathe five breaths into him. I then place my hands on his ribcage and do ten compressions over his heart.

I repeat the process ten times, crying the entire time.

"Wake up," I sob as I start the eleventh repetition.

But as I stare down at him, he doesn't gasp. He doesn't open his eyes. His chest doesn't rise and fall on its own.

"I won't let you stay there," I promise him, anger creeping into my voice. "You don't get to give up on me. You took away my choice once." Black vipers rise up in my blood. "This time I'm taking away yours. I will find a way to bring you back, whether you like it or not."

I take a step back from him, swallowing once.

It's a promise. One I'll move heaven and hell to keep.

So I turn, holding my chin high, and I leave.

CHAPTER 10

WITH SO FEW IN THE CASTLE, BECAUSE I DON'T TRUST anyone right now, it takes a long time to find anyone. I wander through multiple levels, listening for anyone. Finally, on the fourth floor, I hear someone on the far side. Following the noise, I step into a room where Alivia and Ian are quietly talking.

"What's going on?" I ask, probably sharper than necessary.

Alivia looks pale white, like she's going to throw up any minute. Ian doesn't look happy.

"We found him," she says. "We followed him around town for a few hours."

My mouth instantly goes dry.

I know exactly who she's talking about.

My biological father.

"And?" I question. But the word comes out rough and quiet.

Alivia swallows, and when she can't immediately find her words, Ian speaks for her.

"He didn't do anything suspicious," he says. "He went to the tavern. Fed from a feeder. He went to his house, and didn't seem to do anything abnormal for the few hours we watched him."

I kind of hate that. This would be so much easier if he was just obviously up to something. But if he appears normal, it means it will be much more difficult to get clear answers.

"Mina went inside and arrested him," Alivia finishes. "She didn't give him any kind of explanation, just that he was being taken to the castle for eventual questioning."

Eventual. I know what that means. It's a tactic we've used frequently. As immortals, we're rarely in a hurry. But the days are incredibly long when you're locked up in a dungeon. Letting a person sit for an extended period of time makes them confess sooner.

"So, he's here?" I ask.

With a grim set to her lips, Alivia nods.

"He's down in a cell on the lower level," Ian says. "I put him in solitary. We figured we better talk to you first before we decide how to proceed."

I nod, but I feel my vision glaze over a little as my brain runs a million miles a minute.

Meeting Alivia was scary. And I'd at least had a few people tell me a little bit about her. But my biological father? Every single thing about him is unknown, except that he is a Royal vampire.

None of us even know his name.

I wipe my hands on my pants, trying not to be so terrified.

"I want to see him," I say without even thinking about it.

Alivia goes even paler, but Ian nods his head and walks to the door. Hesitantly, Alivia steps to my side and we follow her husband.

"Can I ask," I say as we make our way through the passageways. "Because it's pretty obvious you are. Why are you so terrified?"

Alivia looks over at me, a mix of a glare and surprise in her eyes.

"You just thought it was a hook up, you didn't know what was going on," I say. "You don't know anything about the man as far as you've led me to believe. So why are you so scared?"

My mother, who only looks a year or two older than me, looks away. She shakes her head. "I think it's because of when I saw him again, here in Roter Himmel," she says. "I wasn't…in a good place…in every way, when I saw him again." She seems uncomfortable, unsure how to explain this. "And when I saw him, that's when I realized what it meant for you."

She looks over at me. "I gave you up for adoption because I thought it was best for you, that this was the way I could give you the best life possible. But when I saw him…" She shakes her head. "I knew it meant so many different things, and that it would ruin that normal life I'd tried to give you."

She stares ahead. Even though she is a vampire, an immortal, and all of her instincts make her calm and deadly, her hands shake. "I guess that fear and panic is just coming back from that moment. And there are so many unknowns. I want answers."

"I think you'd be a little nervous, too, if you had to wonder if a man had somehow known what you were long before you did," Ian says as we turn a corner and descend down a flight of stairs.

We walk down a hall and turn into another. It's dark down here. It smells of moisture and despair.

I'm reminded that there are as many occupants in the castle as there are prisoners. There is that group my interrogators collected when trying to vet the kingdom.

Just one more thing I need to deal with.

Finally, we turn down a hall past the entrance to the prison. There is a heavy metal door that Ian swings open. Inside is an interrogation room, much like the one I used before.

I wasn't ready.

I really wasn't.

Not yet.

But just inside, there is a window.

Beyond that is a room.

And sitting inside is a man.

His shoulders are broad and his frame is strong. Sitting down, I can tell he isn't particularly tall, I'd guess around five foot nine. The dark blue t-shirt he wears reveals strong forearms and scarred hands.

His face is covered with thick facial hair that looks like it was shaved about five days ago. Thick, dark brown hair covers his head.

And here, even outside the room, even in the dim light, I can see his eyes.

More yellow than green, they stand out, striking.

They look exactly like mine.

Everything in me snags. Stutters. Hiccups.

Thunder, thunder, beat, beat, beat.

There he is.

The man who made up the other half of my DNA.

And I don't know a single thing about him.

Not his name.

Not if he's a good or evil person.

Nothing whatsoever.

He sits calmly at the table, staring blankly at the wall across from him.

I can't read anything off of him.

"No one has said anything to him since he was brought in?" I ask, staring at the man.

"No," Ian says.

I nod. "And he hasn't said anything?"

He shakes his head.

Once more, I nod.

"It's only been about four hours," Ian says, looking back at the man his wife once slept with. "You said you wanted him to sweat it out for a while."

"Leave him for another twenty-four hours," I say. For just a second, a hitch of panic jumps in my stomach. Because we're on a timeline now, the clock is ticking. "I want both of you to meet me back here, then. We'll get some answers out of him."

I turn and stalk down the hall. Away, putting distance between myself and that man.

I need to talk to someone about this. To go over and over how messed up this is. How I'm a product of a mistake or a manipulation.

But who the hell can I talk to?

Certainly not Eshan. Not when he was abandoned as a baby and left for dead before someone took him to the orphanage.

I can't call Mom or Dad now, not that I could even begin to explain this to them.

Amelia couldn't handle the truth.

All I want is to talk to Cyrus about this.

Anger, hot and vile rips through my blood.

I grab a vase sitting on a side table, and hurl it at the mirror on the wall as I walk past it.

CHAPTER 11

OVER THE NEXT TWENTY-FOUR HOURS, I DO NOT GET TWO seconds to sit down or five minutes to catch my breath.

I find a note from Larkin in my office, saying that he has found the three Born. He has them in a secure location and is implementing persuasive interrogation measures.

My mind rests a little easier knowing all the Born players are either in custody, or dead.

But there's still that spark of doubt in my brain, the one that tells me this extends far beyond just the Born.

I spend over ten million dollars in preparation. Over two thousand years, Cyrus has built up an incredible amount of wealth, but it still feels like a huge hit.

But it will all be worth it if we know we are safe and can trust those around us.

Dorian, Malachi, and I set up camp in Cyrus' office. We lock the doors, and I know the room is soundproof, but still we end up largely talking in whispers. We have maps and spreadsheets spanning across the room. There are timelines drawn up. We review the plan over and over and over.

To execute what we have planned, we should need months. The scope of it is so enormous.

But we don't have that kind of time.

It may already be too late.

Word has already spread around the globe of Cyrus' murder. So many players could be moving against us already.

So the three of us accomplish the impossible in mere hours instead of months.

"They will be here in twenty-six hours," Malachi says when he hangs up the phone.

I look to Dorian, who gives an agreeing nod.

With one last look around the room, I realize that we're done.

We've finished everything we can do. We've got everything in place.

"Then we wait," I say, nodding. "We each know our position to take when they arrive."

There's a weighted moment where no one says anything. So I take a step, headed to the door.

I still have other business to attend to.

"It's madness," Malachi says. "Your plan."

I look back at him, preparing for a protest or a challenge.

"But it's brilliant," he adds. I see awe and respect there in his eyes. "Far more brilliant and beautiful than anything Cyrus would have devised. And in the end, their devotion to you will be one hundred fold. They are going to worship you after this."

I blink. My brain, my eyes, my soul are tired.

But I'm grateful. "Thank you," I say evenly.

Dorian bows to me, agreement reflected in his impressed eyes.

I offer them a small, appreciative smile. It's all I have energy for. And I leave the office.

Because I am Queen. Ruler over this powerful domain that exists in the regular world. And I am far from finished on this evening.

I easily navigate through the castle and turn corner after corner, until finally, there is the interrogation room at the end of the hall, and Ian and Alivia wait there for me.

"What do you have?" I demand, harsher than I should. I only have so much time, and the stress of it all is turning me into a not very pleasant person.

"Mina doesn't know a whole lot about him," Alivia starts. I'm grateful she seems to understand my urgency, even if she has no clue what is coming. "He doesn't often come to the castle, hasn't had much interaction with Cyrus."

"I spoke with two of your first interviewees," Ian says, crossing his arms over his chest. "Apparently, he travels quite a bit. Sounds like he goes around the globe pretty regularly."

"Doing what?" I ask, my brows narrowing.

Ian shrugs. "No one seems to know in particular, but it sounds like he just gets bored and has a case of wanderlust. Live long enough, I can see that happening."

I nod, though it makes me a little uneasy. "What else?"

"His father and mother were killed a long, long time ago," Ian continues. "No one seems to know the details very clearly, but there's something about his father feeding on a human and getting caught. But Lorenzo was only thirteen at the time, so he basically raised himself."

A small pang of sympathy stabs in my stomach.

None of that seems fair.

"He has four children here at Court," Alivia says. I look over to meet her eyes, surprise in both of ours. "They're all over a hundred years Resurrected. From what we can tell they're pretty close, they all live in the same house here in Roter Himmel."

Interesting. I have four biological half siblings.

"Anything else?" I ask as my heartbeat increases.

Ian looks at Alivia and gives a little shake of his head. "That's all we were able to gather in such a short amount of time."

I nod. "Well, at least it's something. Let's get this started."

Alivia looks at her husband, nerves written all over every bit of her body language. But like a mask appears over her face, she composes it. She stands a little straighter. And then two of them step toward the door.

When Ian sets his hand on the knob, my hand darts out, touching his shoulder.

"Wait," I say in a quick breath. They both look back at me. "What's his name?" Goose bumps flash over my arms. "His real name?"

I meet my mother's eyes, and I know, after all these years, how relieved she has to be to finally know it.

"Lorenzo St. Claire," she says.

Ian opens the door, and the two of them step inside,

sitting face to face with the man who keeps running his fingers through his hair.

I swallow once, trying to force down the hard knot in my throat. Crossing my arms over my chest, I stand in front of the one-way mirror, looking into the room, having no idea what to expect.

Ian drags back a seat, immediately sitting across from Lorenzo. But it's him I watch. His face. He looks back and forth from Ian to Alivia, and back to Ian.

I don't see any signs of recognition in his face when he sees my mother.

That seems genuine.

"Sorry about that wait," Ian says, though he doesn't sound sorry in the least. "Things have been a little busy here in the castle as of late."

"Can I ask what I've done?" Lorenzo asks. His voice is hoarse and rough, like he needs a drink.

But the sound of his voice sends goose bumps flashing across my arms.

That's the voice of the other half of my DNA.

And it speaks with an unidentifiable accent.

Slightly German. Maybe a little Italian. I don't even know what the rest is.

But Italian. As I look at him, as I think about my own face, I'd guess that's where his—our roots could be from.

I may look just like Alivia, but as I stare at this man, I'm starting to pick up little traces I got from him. The arch of his brows. His ears. The thickness of my hair. The way we hold our shoulders.

Hell. I've heard six words from his mouth, but I can't deny it. This man *is* my biological father.

"That's what we're not really sure about," Ian answers Lorenzo's question. "But to get right to things, I have to ask: do either of us look familiar to you?"

There's no beating around the bush when it comes to Ian. I raise an eyebrow, impressed with his boldness.

Lorenzo's eyes flick from Ian, over to Alivia, and then back to Ian. "Neither of you is from Court, or I would have recognized you immediately." He studies Ian for a long moment, but I don't see any kind of recognition alight in his eyes.

They then slide over to Alivia, and he studies her longer. His eyes narrow, and I can tell he's wracking his brain.

I watch him, so close. We need to know the truth. We need to be able to tell if he's lying. But I don't see anything masked there. I don't see any hidden stories in his expression.

"You look familiar maybe," he muses, but there's uncertainty on his face. His eyes narrow again, but he shakes his head. "I assume you're associated with one of the Houses. You have that confidence about you. But," he shakes his head again. "I'm sorry, I travel a lot, so there are a lot of faces, you know?"

Damn. I believe he's telling the truth.

Not what I was expecting.

"How long has it been since you last traveled through the state of Colorado in the United States?" Alivia asks.

And I respect her bravery. She just says it. Like she isn't terrified.

Maybe I get some of my salty boldness from her.

"Co..." he trails off, wracking his brain. "Colorado."

And slowly, so slowly that I know he isn't faking it, a light dawns in his eyes.

"Alivia," he pulls her name from the recesses of his memory. He nods. "You...you took your father's place, then?" His eyes are wide, surprised, and there's a spark of... something that lights in them.

"You didn't hear?" Ian asks, doubtful. "It was kind of a big deal when it happened. You didn't notice that King Cyrus was missing for nearly a month?"

Lorenzo's eyes widen a bit but he shakes his head and shrugs. "It's something that's happened a lot over the past 286 years. Life here in Court is different than out there in the world. You don't have to pay attention to all the players quite the same."

"So you knew who I was when you met me, *David Smith*?" Alivia asks with a little bite in her voice.

David Smith. No wonder she was so sure he hadn't given her his real name. It might not have been John Smith, or John Doe, but just as generic.

He doesn't give much of a reaction at being called on lying. He sits forward, looking down at the table. "I didn't realize at first," he says. He draws a little circle on the tabletop with the tip of his finger. "I was traveling through the states at the time, a road trip, I guess. I happened to stop there in Colorado and just kind of...wandered. And ended up at that movie theater."

Alivia looks up at Lorenzo from beneath her lashes. I see

it in her face: the embarrassment and shame over whatever happened that night.

"But as we got talking, as you told me about your mom, the connections to Mississippi, you suddenly started to look familiar. Like a man I had once met at Court, a really long time ago."

Alivia's face hardens, and her eyes darken.

But Lorenzo's soften. "But as we kept talking, it became apparent that you had no idea who Henry Conrath was. That you didn't know what I was. I had no way to be one hundred percent sure that you were Henry's daughter, but I suspected."

"Is that the reason you slept with her?" Ian asks. There's so much bite to his voice, and I can see it: it won't take much to make Ian snap.

Lorenzo studies Ian. His lips are set thin, his jaw clenched tight. His hands curl into fists. And I can't blame him. I don't like it when Ian comes slinging hot, hard words at me, either.

"I'll admit," he says, looking up at Alivia. "I was curious. But that night wasn't all a lie, Alivia. You were…" he shrugs, his eyes dropping to the table surface again. "Sweet. And charming. And I hadn't laughed like that in a long time. So what ended up happening that night, don't think it was fake."

I can see from Alivia's expression that with everything in her, she does, though. She looks sick. Absolutely humiliated.

I place my hand on the knob and pull the door open. With absolute confidence I step into the room and cross to the table.

Lorenzo sits back in his chair, his golden jade-colored

eyes widening as he looks at me, his mouth opens, but no words come out.

"Answer me honestly," I say as I place my palms flat on the table and lean in toward him. "Did you sleep with Alivia, suspecting she was a Royal, as an experiment to see if you could conceive me?"

Lorenzo's eyes flick back and forth between the two of mine, and I know he sees it. They're the exact same as his own. They're unique and unmistakable. And my face, it looks so much like my mother's.

"I..." he stutters. "Yes, I was curious what would happen, but it wasn't all about that." He's panicking, but also looks... in awe. "I did go back nine months later, though. But when I went back, when I found Alivia again, there was no baby."

Still, Alivia has no words. She just stares at Lorenzo, a look of betrayal and disgust on her face.

"Look," he says sitting forward, his eyes wide and imploring as he looks at me. "My parents were taken from me when I was young. I was on my own, had to make all the hard calls myself. Growing up in this town on my own wasn't easy. I've always wanted a family. I have four children here, and yes, I wanted more. I thought maybe, if Alivia had gotten pregnant, maybe I could tell her what she was, and we could have taken the baby back here, and then someday Alivia would have been immortal, and it would have been perfect."

There's hope in his expression. Longing.

I just can't tell if it's fake.

"But when I returned to Colorado, and there was no baby, I was disappointed," he says. "No baby. And maybe she wasn't Henry Conrath's daughter, after all. She was still leading a normal, human life. So I moved on."

"So, we have learned you're no real gentleman," I say, staring him down. "You hoped she was pregnant, but you weren't going to stick around during the pregnancy and be any kind of support. You're obviously a strong family man."

My blood is hot, and I can tell my eyes have ignited red.

Lorenzo just stares at me, and he doesn't have a response to that.

It kind of makes me want to spit in his face.

"But I suppose I should be grateful that you were such a curious and charmed man," I move on, feeling the familiar acid rise in my blood. "Because you slept with Alivia, and nine months later, I was born, and placed with a wonderful adoptive family. So I guess I should thank you."

But my expression only hardens, and black ink saturates my veins.

"Eight months and three and a half weeks," Alivia says. "Logan was born a week and a half early."

Which explains why when Lorenzo returned to Colorado to check on Alivia, there were no signs of a baby. She'd already given birth, and I'd already been placed with my family in Greendale.

"It's curious, and I'm sure Cyrus would have been very interested to test it back when," I say, continuing to stare my father down. "A Royal and a female Royal *before* she Resurrects. Would it always bring the Queen back?"

And suddenly, as if he's just remembered who I am, he bows his head, nearly touching his forehead to the table.

"I hope you don't mind being a guest at the castle for a

little while longer," I say as I straighten, standing. Alivia and Ian stand as well and we all three walk to the door. "We may have more questions. I think we should get to know each other a little better." I look back over my shoulder just before I walk out. "Father."

It makes my skin crawl, calling him that. But I'm also playing a mind game here, and when his face pales considerably, I know I've succeeded.

We close the door behind us, locking Lorenzo inside once more.

Together, we walk down the hall.

"So, is he lying?" Ian asks.

I walk straight ahead, not looking back. I still am not finished on this night.

"Honestly, the last twenty minutes are a little bit of a hazy red blur," Alivia says, her voice hard and icy. "All I could think was *manipulator*."

"I really don't think he recognized you at first, Alivia," I state my opinions. "It's been nearly twenty-one years since he last saw you, and you aged another…four years after he saw you, so you probably do look a little different."

We round a corner and start up a staircase.

"Everything he said is logical, I would say. And he admitted he was curious about what would happen between two Royals." We level out onto the fourth floor. "What I wonder is if he is holding any information back."

"Like what?" Ian asks.

We step onto the main level and I suddenly stop. "I don't know," I say, staring down the long hallway, once again feeling drained and overwhelmed. I turn back, looking at Ian and Alivia. "You've done what I asked you to come here and do," I say. I look to Alivia, who watches me warily now. "Thank you. I know it wasn't easy coming here. You..." I hesitate for some reason. "You can go home now. Your House needs you."

Alivia's brows furrow. She takes a step forward. "Logan, you're going through...an insane amount of pressure. You don't know who to trust. Cyrus is...we don't now what's going to happen to him. My House is just fine, Logan. You need our help, and you're going to take it."

She's determined. I see that she means it and she isn't going to back down.

Which makes me feel even more tired, because I know what's about to come. And I know I have no choice but to let the both of them get wrapped up in the chaos I'm about to unleash on Roter Himmel.

"Okay," I say.

Without another word, I turn and head up the stairs.

CHAPTER 12

IN MY BEDROOM, I CHANGE INTO NONDESCRIPT CLOTHES. I braid my hair over one shoulder and pull on a hat. On my way to the entry of the castle, I make a detour. Down to the fourth floor. Through a passageway. And then a huge space opens up.

It's the size of a ballroom, but there isn't anything in it. The stone floors stretch out before me. Three of the walls are unadorned. The room is plain, really.

But I turn to the fourth wall, and a feeling of...immenseness washes over me.

There is a mural on this wall. It's massive considering the ceiling stretches twenty, maybe twenty-five feet high, and a hundred feet wide.

Painted over seventeen hundred years ago, it is a massive family tree.

At the top is mine and Cyrus' names. Just below that was

our sons', but it's now covered with angry black paint streaks, forever crossed out from our history.

Below that there are all of our grandchildren, each of their names blotted out as well, with the exception of Dorian and Malachi.

Every one of their children branches off from them. So many names, so many faces I can recall.

There are each and every one of my fathers throughout time. Helda's. Edith's. La'ei's.

Our DNA may be far scattered, with such variation you'd have to dig deep to find the common denominator of Cyrus and I. But here's the evidence. That we're all connected, we're all family in some distant way.

I feel the two voices inside myself in awe. Logan is amazed, overwhelmed at the size and spread of all of these blood descendants.

Sevan feels such a surge of love and protection for them. These are her heirs. The result of a terrifying night of stripped-away will, and then a few years of being a happy, though complicated, family.

I clutch my hands to my heart as I search this wall, taking in all of the names that have been added through time.

With a breath, I turn, and head back through the castle. I walk out the front gates onto the road that leads straight down into the town.

It's a quiet night. Despite the fact that it's beautiful weather, warm and comfortable, not a cloud in the sky, there aren't many people out. It's dark now, the beginning of our day. But the streets aren't filled. Most seem to still be in their homes.

The shops are quiet as I pass them. The eateries are largely unoccupied.

I don't mind. It's less risk I will be spotted. It means I can just reflect on our town that Cyrus and I built together.

I walk down the road and hit the tee at the lake's edge. To the right it rounds the lake, more homes and businesses set off to the side of it, and eventually it goes to the canyon that is the main outlet to the outside world.

To the left, it cuts toward the fields and farms that support the town. The homes are spread out further.

There is a trail that loops around the lake, and it's to that I set my course.

I think back as I walk. To what this place was when Cyrus and I first arrived. It was covered in snow. The remaining buildings had been toppled, the homes burned to the ground. The castle still stood, but it had been mostly gutted.

We learned centuries later that this town had been invaded once and the inhabitants killed.

No one had ever come back to reclaim it. No one ever traveled the road our direction. Roter Himmel is remote, over an hour's drive to the nearest town. We are not located on any map. So here, we have been safe for centuries.

But all that is threatened now.

I feel like a greedy king as I pull myself up onto a large rock at the lake's edge. Cyrus and I have ruled for a long, long time. Maybe someone else would do a better job. Would be a better ruler.

But after doing things our way for so long, it's nearly

impossible to give up control. I could never, ever trust someone else to lead us and to protect our kind.

"Did you ever want more?" I asked Cyrus as we walked along this same river's edge. My hand was in his, his grip strong and secure.

"More what?" Cyrus asked me to clarify.

I looked at him, wearing Shaku's face. "More children? I know it was an impossibility, but did you ever think about it?"

He looked out at the trail ahead of us, his eyes going dark. "There was too much to think about in those early days to wish for more than just our son," he said. "Between our changes, between running for our lives, no, I never thought about more children."

I looked over at the man I'd loved with four different faces now. "It is still possible," I say, but my words came out quiet. "We know for a fact that you could take a human woman. You could still have more children if you wanted, Cyrus."

He pulled me to a stop, stepping in front of me so that our faces were very close together. His brows furrowed. "The only thing I desire any longer is to be with you, Sevan. And how could I ever think I would make a good father, after what became of our son?"

I reached up and laced my fingers into his hair. "I have to believe that we come into this world with our own ideas and desires. I do not think what happened to our son was entirely because of us."

Cyrus reached up, palming my jaw and brushing his thumb over my cheek. "Let me be very clear, im yndmisht srtov. I have never wanted more children. I would never, ever lie with another woman. You and I, it is all I have ever wanted. And what we have built here?" He looks up, his eyes searching for the small town off in the distance. "This is our legacy. All of these people here. They are our family. They are our blood. And I have never wanted anything more."

I smiled as I looked up into his face.

Cyrus was so passionate whenever he spoke. I always believed every word he spoke, because of the way he said the words. With such conviction.

"I love you," I breathed as I leaned in and kissed him.

"And I love you, Sevan."

I tuck my knees into my chest, hugging them tight. The air feels cold now. There is no body hugged to mine to keep me warm. There's just me, on this rock, in this incredible town that I love.

I look back on it now, and my heart feels heavy. Because come morning, during the brightest part of the day, every one of these descendants of mine will quake in fear, thinking the end has arrived.

CHAPTER 13

THEY COME IN THE MIDDLE OF THE DAY. WEARING A SET OF sunshades, I go to the window in my room and look out over the valley nestled between the mountains.

Like ants, black dots slip silently through the canyon. They spill out into the green grass floors of Roter Himmel. I'm truly impressed at their silence as they creep closer and closer to town. There are so many of them. Their footsteps should send a rumble into the air like the sound of a stampede.

But they're soundless as they flood into the town.

I watch as they surround every single home while my people rest inside, oblivious to what I'm about to do to them.

The horde stretches up the road.

Holding my head high, I step out of my room, and work my way down through the castle. Dorian and Malachi are waiting for me on the main floor. We give one another a silent look, our expressions grave.

We understand the weight of what we're about to do.

But there is no other way.

I step forward, crossing the entry. With one last breath, I pull the doors open.

Three hundred soldiers, each of them bearing the Austrian crest on their uniforms, rush forward, flooding into the castle. Two of them roughly grab me, yanking my hands behind my back and handcuffing me. They do the same to Malachi and Dorian. The other soldiers spill into the castle, heading for every crevice and room in the castle.

The ones they can find, anyway.

I look to my grandsons again, and their faces are calm but worried.

Just two minutes later, shouts, screams, and protests fill the air, coming from every direction. Outside in the town, from down the halls of the castle.

You have to pretend now, I tell myself. They have to believe it.

"No!" I scream, fighting against the men who have cuffed me. "We've done nothing wrong! You cannot just invade us like this!"

I pour every ounce of vile acid I have in me into my words. I lunge and buck, and four more guards throw themselves at me.

Just in time. Because just then, soldiers drag Ian, Alivia, Eshan, and some of the other prisoners into the hall.

They're battered. Bruised. Cuts line their fists and faces.

But every one of them is cuffed with four or five guards handling them.

"Cooperate, or she dies," one of my guards bellows. He grabs me roughly, holding a huge blade to my throat.

"Logan!" Alivia screams, her eyes wild. There's a huge gash on her cheek and blood slips down her face.

"What the hell is going on?" Ian demands, struggling against the six men who hold him under their control.

"I don't know!" I cry, my muscles automatically twitching, trying to keep that blade from slicing my throat. "Just... do what they say! I don't want anyone to get hurt! We'll figure this out."

Soldiers drag Lorenzo out into the hall and I meet his eyes for just a moment before my own soldiers drag me toward the front doors.

I brace for the pain. Because to sell this, I had to take my sunshades off before I came down the stairs.

They shove me forward, and I stumble out into the blindingly brilliant summer sun.

A scream rips from my lips, and it's one hundred percent genuine. Pain rips through my head, burning my eyes. I'm blind. There's so much sun and my eyes remain so permanently dilated, all I can see is white and fuzzy orbs.

I want to rip my eyeballs from my head.

My brain is melting. I swear I taste steel and copper in the back of my throat.

There are endless screams of pain around me. I blink furiously, trying to force my eyes to clear as the soldiers roughly shove me down the road and toward the middle of town.

My vision clears. Not much. But to where I can somewhat make sense of the fuzzy shapes around me.

Here, down the road, every resident of Roter Himmel has been herded into the middle of the street. Four hundred vampires, forced outside in the blinding midday sun.

Surrounding them, there are rows and rows of soldiers. Human, every one of them. But heavily armed.

There are six thousand of them. There are four hundred of us.

They outnumber us fifteen to one.

Down the road they force me and as I approach, I see bloodshot eyes turn my way. Looks of fear and panic deepen on their faces.

I am their Queen. And here I am, a bound prisoner, just as they are.

"Sevan!" some of them shout. Some of them jerk against their bonds. Some reach out to me. Some cry.

Others shout vile things at me. Accusations about not protecting the town.

Everyone is terrified.

The rest of us who were in the castle are shoved into a herd and the ring of soldiers tightens around us, guns all pointed at us.

We're strong. We're fast.

But outnumbered fifteen to one, with all those assault weapons? We don't stand a chance.

I look around at my people, trembling.

I really am scared.

Because this looks even better than I planned it.

A man beside me mutters, over and over, his words hardly even comprehensible. Something about bad omens.

As I look around, I see a mix of reactions.

In some faces, I see a daring look, and my anxiety reaches near heart-stopping peaks, because I know what will happen if they really do try to fight their way through this.

But on others, I see terror. Most of them here were never part of those early wars with my son. Most of them here have never had to fight for anything.

I realize now how soft everyone at Court has grown.

"It was a bad omen," the man mutters again. "Foretelling of darkness. The sun overtaken by the dark."

Something pricks at the back of my brain.

Words.

Words spoken in sleep. Spoken in dreams.

"The darkness during the light," the man says.

I turn, looking at his face. He has his eyes closed, his face turned toward the sky, despite the burning sun above us.

"What do you mean?" I breathe. Because suddenly I remember. I remember that first dream I had of Cyrus, when he was so frantic, saying that we must prepare. Talking about the dark during the light. "The darkness during the light? What are you talking about?"

The man's eyes slide open. They're absolutely bloodshot, and it's a horrifying sight. "It was a bad omen," he says cryptically. "We should have known something dark was coming. For the first time in over two hundred years, the dark will overtake the light in Roter Himmel."

I feel cold and twisted. "I don't understand," I whisper.

The man's eyes grow wider slowly and he raises a hand to chest height, and points to the sun. "Exactly as the astrologists predicted. The day after tomorrow, the dark will take over the light."

"A solar eclipse," I breathe as a million lights turn on in my head.

A shot fires into the air, and I instinctually duck slightly, covering my head. All the screams and cries fall silent, and every set of eyes turns just to the south.

On the balcony of a house, just past the ring of vampires, a man stands, looking over us all.

His gaze cuts. He stares down, a look of absolute disgust on his face.

His hair is a dark blond. His lips have a slightly pinched look to them, making him look like he's always thinking about something serious. A strong body is framed in an intimidating uniform. I'd say he's not much over thirty years old.

"My name is General Matthias Reiter," he says loudly over the quieting crowd. "On behalf of the Republic of Austria, I am placing all of you under arrest for the murder of over six thousand residents of our country."

Confused whispers billow into the air, frightened, blood-shot eyes searching one another for answers.

"This will be a thorough investigation," Matthias says, his eyes darkening even further. "I hope you are all comfort-able. The country of Austria wants some answers, and this may take some time."

Soldiers shove their way to me once more, roughly grab-bing me and dragging me to the outside of the circle.

Those around me grab at my arms, trying to keep me from the soldiers. But when big guns are shoved into their faces, they let go, panic in their eyes as they watch me be dragged away.

"Please cooperate!" I bellow as they drag me through the crowd. "But never forget the promises we must keep to our own!"

My words are cut off as I am dragged into a building, and the doors swing closed with a slam.

The crowd outside goes insane, shouts and screams and rioting.

I hear one gunshot, and everything goes quieter.

I pray that one of my own isn't lying dead on the street because of my choice.

"This is quite a ruse you've pulled off here." A voice cuts through the home I was pulled into. I hear footsteps and see booted feet descend the stairs just off to my left.

From the shadows at the back of the house, Dorian and Malachi step forward, rubbing their wrists as soldiers release them.

"You certainly fill the part well," I say. A soldier releases my own bonds and I straighten my clothes.

Matthias gives me a little smile and stops just in front of me.

He fits the part so perfectly, I nearly believe he actually is a General in the Republic of Austria.

"We will make sure no one sees you go back to the castle," he says. "As far as the public knows, you're being held here, undergoing extreme interrogation measures."

I nod in acknowledgement and turn to my grandsons. "They look perfect." And a smile slowly grows on my face.

Outside there are six thousand soldiers, far outnumbering

the residents of Roter Himmel. Every one of them looks the part of a soldier in the Austrian army.

But they're all fake.

True, most of them actually are soldiers.

But they come from Dorian and Malachi's own private armies.

Dorian rules all of Russia. His reign is vast and he could never keep it under control without some real force.

Malachi has always allied himself with real political power. One phone call and multiple governments turned over sections of their special force armies.

Combined, with faked uniforms and illegal weapons, they look the part of an Austrian army.

"The interrogations will begin today," Matthias says, stepping forward. He eyes me up and down, his gaze slightly too appreciative. There's a dark look in his eye.

"Take your time," I say. "Let them panic. Let them get scared. Let them have time to consider how outnumbered they are."

Let them realize how fragile we as a species really are when there are so few of us.

The entire goal here is to reiterate how important keeping our kind secret really is.

Above all else, Cyrus valued secrecy. Because he had been hunted before. He knew what could happen to us if the general public knew about us.

They all need to understand that fear.

"Of course, your majesty," Matthias says. Locking his dark eyes on mine, he takes a deep bow.

He is from Russia, but his accents and German are

impeccable. One would never, ever guess that he was not born and raised in this country.

Dorian trusts him implicitly. He has a massive role to play. And thus far, I do believe he will rise to the occasion.

"Don't let me down," I say.

With a smile, he straightens.

I turn toward the back doors where a wagon waits, where I will hide for a while, before a soldier takes it away, and then I will sneak my way back to the castle.

I stop between Dorian and Malachi as I walk between them. I place a hand on either of their shoulders.

"Thank you," I say, looking at each of them. "Over and over you have proved your loyalty to this family, and it will never, ever be forgotten. None of this would have been possible without your help."

I will go back to the castle. But Dorian and Malachi will stay here, working with Matthias in rooting out any who might betray our kind.

"Anything, All Mother," Dorian says as he kisses my hand that sits on his shoulder.

"You have my loyalty until the day I die," Malachi promises with determination in his eyes. He hands me a pair of sunshades.

I smile, my heart filled to the brim with appreciation and love.

With a deep breath, I step forward and slip the sunshades on. A soldier holds the back door open for me.

I step into the small garden out back. Soldiers keep lookout and wave me forward. A wagon waits behind the shed, and I climb into what appears to be a cargo box.

It's cramped and utterly pitch black, but after the searing pain of having to walk outside, it's a relief.

As planned, I wait for over an hour. And finally, the box lurches, and I feel it dragged forward by the horses. And a soldier takes me back to the castle.

CHAPTER 14

I BURST THROUGH THE CASTLE DOORS TO A PERFECTLY SILENT and very nearly empty space. With invisible speed, I dart through the hallways. Just seconds later, I shove the doors open to Cyrus' office and go straight for the computer on the desk against the far wall.

Opening it, I do some quick Internet searching. I check, and double and triple check that I'm reading from credible sources.

"Holy shit," I breathe, my eyes flicking over the information just one more time.

The seemingly mad-sounding man was right.

For the first time in over two hundred years, there will be a total solar eclipse, centered right over Roter Himmel. Total coverage, total darkness during the middle of the day.

At 1:11 in the afternoon, to be exact.

I am searching for the way back. So we must prepare. You

must be ready. It will be soon, when the day is dark as the night.

We have to prepare. We must be ready.

I sit back, recalling that strange dream, that vision. *Remember*, I yell at myself. *Every detail. He was showing you exactly what must be done.*

Darting to my feet, I head out of the office.

The ceremony from the dream was done outside, out in an open space, where the sun would reach every part of the circle. There is a field above the castle, tucked far out of sight of the village where there will be no risk of the residents seeing us.

I head out to the courtyard, to the storage facility. There, I find a huge cache of cut wood. By the armload, I load it up, and make the trek up the trail that rises up the back of the castle. Exactly as I remember Cyrus doing from the dream, I place them in a wide circle, taking care that they line up end to end.

It takes me five trips to gather enough wood.

With my sunshades still securely on as I work, I close my eyes as I stand in the middle of the circle, pulling back to memory every detail of the dream.

An altar in the center. The fragrant herbs burning along with the wood.

Through the entire day, I work by myself. I build that altar. I think back to the way those herbs smelled, trying to identify which ones he used. Through the kitchens and the infirmary I dig, searching for them.

I scatter the herbs along the logs.

I'm going to have to prepare well ahead of time. In the

dream, Cyrus already had the logs burning. When the sky grew dark, they'd been smoldering for quite some time. I will need to light the fires at least an hour before the peak of the eclipse.

Crazy, crazy, this is crazy, Logan says in the back of my brain. *None of this is real. You've seen a partial eclipse before and while it was cool, there was* nothing *magic about it.*

But Sevan remembers all the stories Cyrus told her about his family. Mud healers and star worshipers, he'd called them. She had seen him look to the stars himself, seen his lips move in silent prayers and pleas. She knows there is more to the skies than beauty.

I'm filthy when I finally finish. Excited and tired and doubtful but hopeful, I stand in the center of my circle as the sun slips down past the mountains to the west, draping me once more in comfortable darkness.

For a moment, I listen. Sound carries far in Roter Himmel, in this valley and with that huge lake.

All throughout the day, there has been shouts and commands and cries. But now, as the sun has finally set and my people have relief, it's quieter. They've been separated, taken to different buildings, and I know the uncertainty they must feel right now.

But it's necessary. We have to find who will betray us, who has begun thinking in the old ways.

I take one last look around the circle, sure that everything is perfectly prepared. Goosebumps flash across my skin as I think about what will happen here in less than two days.

I'm scared. Scared that it won't work. That my dream was just that: a dream.

But I have to believe.

What else can I do?

Wiping my dirty hands on my pants, I set back down the now well-traveled path that leads back down to the castle.

It's so quiet. The castle feels cold and empty as I walk through its hallways back to my bedroom.

But I'm relieved.

For the past week, I've been under constant stress and dealing with issue after issue.

It's been taken care of now. I've done everything I could possibly do.

And now I can focus on myself. On Cyrus.

I take nearly an hour washing myself in our bathroom. I dig the dirt from under my fingernails, scrub my streaked hair. I scrub my skin raw and pink.

I pull on a silky nightgown and braid my hair over my shoulder. Looking myself in the mirror one last time, I note how tired I look. I may be an immortal, a vampire with preserved skin and eternally stuck at twenty years old, but I look worn. There are dark bags beneath my eyes. My cheekbones protrude sharply—I realize I've hardly eaten a thing since arriving in Roter Himmel. There is no color to my lips.

That's the reality. I'm exhausted. In every single way.

But in two days that's all going to get better, I tell myself. Everything will fall into place, and then I can finally take two seconds to breathe.

With a sigh, I turn away from my reflection. I grab a

blanket from the basket beside the bed, and set off through the castle once more.

The secret door to the lab opens up and I step inside, lighting the torches. With heavy feet, I cross the space, coming to Cyrus' side.

I haven't checked on him in over twenty-four hours now. But nothing has changed.

Cyrus is healed. His body looks just as attached as the first day I met him in Greendale or the first time I saw him at a dusty market in a country far away. His eyes are closed, his lips shut. He looks as if he is sleeping.

"I understand now," I say, pushing my fingers through his hair. I bend down, pressing my lips to his forehead. "Everything is prepared, just as you showed me. Now all we have to do is wait."

I climb up onto the table with him, once more tucking myself under his arm, resting my head on his chest. I pull the blanket over us, and I let myself imagine the moment he will open his eyes.

CHAPTER 15

AFTER A LONG DAY AND A LONGER NIGHT, I GATHER CYRUS up into my arms. I don't worry about his head falling off anymore. He's solid. Reattached. But still, I'm careful. Just like he was sleeping and I don't want to wake him up.

Through the castle we travel. With sunshades on, I step out into the brilliant sun.

We climb the stone steps that rise up the back of the castle to the clearing. The air grows thick as we get closer, and there's a taste to it. Sweet, bitter.

The logs smoke heavily as I cross the clearing with Cyrus. Set in their perfect circle, they burn and smolder. The smoke is so thick I can hardly see more than three feet in front of me.

I step over the line. Gently, I lay Cyrus on the stone alter. I straighten his legs, lay his arms straight at his sides.

My first instinct is to fold them over his chest. But that is what I did with the dead.

Cyrus is not dead.

Cupping my hands on the sides of his face, I straighten his neck. But I just study him for a long moment.

He seems so peaceful. And for a moment, I feel guilty for forcing him back into this life. There is so much turmoil happening now. So much about our world could change.

Cyrus has done this all for so long. He is finally getting some rest.

But it's my turn to be selfish.

I want him back.

Early this morning, I changed Cyrus clothes. There was still blood all over his previous ones. So I took some from our bedroom and carefully changed him into black jeans and a light blue button up.

I'm wearing a matching light blue dress. Thin straps wrap over my shoulders, the skirt hangs loose around my knees. My hair is curled, half of it tied back behind my head.

This has to be perfect.

Everything will be perfect.

Just like something out of a fairy tale.

It flashes through my brain for a minute, how these events will be retold decades down the line. How Cyrus was finally killed, how it was finally Sevan's turn to fight for Cyrus.

Our legend will grow tenfold.

But first, this has to work.

I straighten, looking around. The logs continue to burn. A weak spot to the south draws me, and I carefully set another in the line. I add more herbs to the east side, making the smoke a pale green for a few minutes.

I nearly choke on the scent of the air.

But as I turn in a circle, observing, it's perfect. Everything looks exactly like it did in the vision Cyrus gave me.

Checking the time on an old timepiece Cyrus used to carry with him everywhere that I brought with me, I see it's exactly one o'clock.

Eleven minutes.

Each one of them feels like a full day.

So I stand beside Cyrus and close my eyes, listening.

Voices float across the valley, but they aren't loud. It's calm, or at least it sounds calm. I know it isn't really down there, where six thousand soldiers question and detain my four hundred descendants here in Roter Himmel.

Guilt rips through my veins. But I swallow once. I did what I had to.

There. Subtle, but so obvious to a vampire, I feel it. A drop in temperature.

I pull on the special glasses, and look to the sun.

A small crescent cuts into the side of the sun that is my most powerful enemy. It slowly, slowly creeps across it.

It's amazing really. That something as powerful as the sun can be overtaken by something as tiny as the moon, even if only for a brief amount of time.

As vampires, one of the biggest things that separates us from the humans we once were, is that we can no longer enjoy the sun. We cannot be out during the day without extreme pain.

If anything can guide a vampire soul back to his body, it is this power.

The air grows cooler and my heart rate triples.

Turning, I stand over Cyrus.

"It is time, *im yndmisht srtov*," I say. My voice trembles. I'm scared. I'm so scared. What if this doesn't work? "Wherever you are, it is time to come back to me. After all these years of separation, now is our time. Come back to me."

The world fractionally grows dimmer. The temperature continues to drop. I look up at the sun once more with my special glasses.

Half of the sun is covered by the moon.

I look at the time again. 1:09.

"Please give him back to me," I beg as I turn my face up to the sky. "There will never be anyone else I can turn to. I have never and will never love another like I love him."

The sky grows dimmer and the air continues to grow colder.

"He has made mistakes, over and over," I tell the universe, the sun, the moon. "But this is a good man. And the world needs him."

Silently, I stand, feeling a heavy darkness press down on me.

Dimmer, dimmer. Darker and darker the world grows.

And finally, I feel it.

The world surrounding me goes dark.

The night during the day.

I remove my eclipse glasses as I look down at Cyrus.

He lies there without moving. His chest does not rise or fall. His fingers do not twitch.

I set my glasses on the altar beside him. The air shifts, blowing the smoke into us and I inhale, tasting the bitter sweet.

116

Through the darkness, my eyes can see him.

"Cyrus," I whisper. "It is time to come back."

I tremble. I'm a quivering leaf as I stare at him so hard I could burn holes right through him.

Open your eyes, I silently plea.

But he's utterly still.

Total darkness. I feel it.

Now. Now is the time.

I feel the seconds ticking. Ticking, ticking until they're gone and the sun will once more take over the moon and the earth.

"Cyrus," I say, my voice growing frantic. Tears prick the backs of my eyes. "Please wake up, Cyrus. I need you to come back to me!"

Fractionally, the worst feeling I've ever felt creeps over my skin. I feel the temperature rise just a degree.

Panic stricken, I pull the timepiece out and check.

1:12.

"No," I breathe, shaking my head. "No. Cyrus. Cyrus, please wake up!"

This is it. If this does not work, I have no other options. I don't know what else to do.

"Cyrus, please!" I cry. I take his face between my hands, shaking him just slightly. All of my insides are trembling. I feel sick. I feel empty. "Cyrus, come back to me!"

But he does not move.

He does not pull in air.

His feet do not twitch.

I die inside.

Everything in me sinks.

The fire inside of me flickers.

"Please," I whisper as I lower down to him. "Come back to me, *im yndmisht srtov*. I love you, Cyrus."

I press my lips to his.

This is the last spark I have.

The last time I will ever feel hope.

So I linger, before I die the death of my soul.

The temperature rises another degree.

And then my hair is ruffled. A hand laces into my hair before cupping the back of my head.

Lips warm and press to mine.

A breath draws in, desperate, pulling me in.

A sound escapes my lungs and a cry becomes a hungry moan as I pull him tighter to my face, to my kiss.

Cyrus pushes himself up onto an elbow but never once breaks the kiss. He holds me closer. His lips part slightly. He tastes of time and immortality and power and pain.

I climb onto the altar, straddling him, never once letting go.

"Cyrus," I weep, scared to open my eyes and find that this is only my imagination.

"Sevan," he says my name. His hand cups the side of my neck, his thumb tracing away the tears pouring down my face. "I'm here, Logan."

And now my eyes finally open.

I have to see if it is real.

He looks at me with those green eyes. Eyes as dark and deep as the forests that surround us.

They look at me with perfect clarity. Scared and tired perhaps, but so utterly solid and real.

"Cyrus," I breathe again, touching my forehead to his. I can't stop the tears of gratitude that slip down my face without stopping. I weep.

"I'm here, my love," he says, gathering me into his arms as I straddle him. "You found me." He whispers into my hair. "You found me."

I tuck my face into his neck and cry and cry. I wrap my arms around his back, hugging him so tight to me that if he were human, he'd be crushed.

And for just a moment, I question.

Cyrus has never died before. He has never gone through a Resurrection.

What if...

I back up just a little, looking into his eyes.

"Are you..." I don't even know what to ask. My lips tremble, and I'm so scared. Because what if I'm still alone? "The cure?"

Cyrus traces his eyes over me, his eyes rising over my neck. Over my lips. And finally to my eyes.

His own flash red dimly. "Nothing has changed, my love," he breathes. "I will always be here for you, until the end of time."

His words break me.

After weeks of separation, after so much longing and arguing with myself, here we are. Together.

Our eyes lock together. I melt. I fuse. My soul with his.

There were so many mistakes made in the past. So much darkness. So many angry words.

But right here, I feel it from my lips, to my stomach, to the very tips of my toes.

I love this man.

I will die for this man.

Over and over. And over and over, I will love him until the sun burns out.

"Cyrus," I breathe, capturing everything coursing through me in one single word.

Cyrus.

I capture his face between my hands and bring my lips to his again.

They are so gentle. Reverent even. Cyrus' lips are permanently impressed to the shape of mine.

He drags his hand up my thigh, sliding under my dress, and cupping my hipbone. His fingers are strong, possessive. Marking me as his own.

My own hands slide up his arms, my fingers digging deep.

His lips part and his tongue gently prods at mine. I let him in willingly, eager to taste him.

A blissful moan escapes my lips.

After all this time. After all the fantasies night after night as I was captive in his newly bought home, after watching him and wondering how he would feel, here we are.

"Logan," he whispers against my flesh. His kisses trail from my lips, over my jaw, down my throat.

I moan, filled with ecstasy.

I tilt my head back, feeling weak with my longing for more, more, more.

But as my eyes slide open, I find the world a dim gray.

The sun is once more overtaking the day. It will be brilliantly bright once more in a matter of minutes.

I sit forward, lacing my fingers into Cyrus' hair. He continues kissing my neck, his breathing a quiver.

"We need to get inside, Cyrus," I say, and it has never been harder to speak words I did not want to say. "The sun will reappear soon."

Like he's just now realized that we are even outside, Cyrus' gaze snaps skyward. I can't read the expression on his face. Awe. Wonder. Disgust. Disappointment.

Cyrus always discounted his family's star worshiping.

And here he is. Finally returned by the power of the cosmos.

"Come," I say. Regretfully, I climb off of him and down from the altar. I take his hand, pulling him to a sitting position and then to his feet.

I step toward the path that leads back to the castle.

But Cyrus stops, pulling me to a halt with him.

The wind has shifted, blowing the smoke back toward the mountain. It clears the view, and the entire valley of Roter Himmel opens up before us.

We can see everything from up here.

The homes. The old church.

And the countless tents pitched. The thousands of bodies milling about.

A look of horror fills Cyrus' face. He turns pale white. His body trembles.

"It's alright, my love," I say, squeezing his hand. "That was me. All of this was my doing."

He blinks once, his mouth slightly slack. But he blinks again, even if he's still pale white.

But he closes his mouth. He swallows once.

So I pull him behind me again. I guide us back down the path that leads to the side door. The world around us grows brighter by the moment.

The pain just begins to stab at the back of my brain when we step into the safety of the castle, and I close the door firmly behind us.

CHAPTER 16

"THE CASTLE IS COMPLETELY EMPTY," I SAY AS WE STEP through the room and enter the hallway. Cyrus' brows furrow, looking around in confusion. "It's just us here. It will be for a little while."

He swallows once and nods. I can see there are a million questions in his eyes. But now is not the time, and that is not what either of us wants to talk about.

"Let's get you to a shower," I say. The confusion in his eyes, the uncertainty, and the exhaustion, they break my heart.

What has he just gone through?

"Cyrus," I say softly. I reach out for his hand, taking it in mine. Gently, I pull him behind me.

We work our way through the castle. We rise up two floors. And down the hall.

There, at the end of it, I see the giant doors to our bedroom.

What am I ready for? What does us being here, in our space, finally together, mean?

My heart beats rapidly.

My palms sweat.

But I can only be grateful. We have so much to figure out. But at least we're here.

At least Cyrus is not dead.

I push the doors open and we step inside. Because I'm scared and I don't even know where to begin, I go straight for the bathroom and start the water in the enormous shower. I turn it hot, testing the water for a moment.

"I'll find you something to wear," I say, turning to Cyrus.

There's a confused, empty look in his eyes.

And I can't blame him.

He may have just come back from the dead.

"You go ahead and shower," I say, explaining things in very simple terms. "I'll be waiting for you in the bedroom."

He blinks twice and nods, stepping into the bathroom.

I'm a ball of nerves as I step out, shutting the door behind me. I'm trembling as I go to the closet, gathering clothing for Cyrus. Mindlessly, I gather things, not really paying attention to what I grab. Without looking, I open the door to the bathroom slightly, laying the clothing on the counter, and exiting once more.

Nervously, I pace the bedroom.

So much anticipation.

I've imagined this day for over a week now, really, for multiple lifetimes. But now that it's here, now that we've had our grand, epic moment of him opening his eyes, now that we've shared our first kiss as Logan and Cyrus, I don't know what to do from here.

Do we just go about living as husband and wife? King and Queen?

I'm terrified of that idea.

I'm just Logan. I've never been married. I've never even had sex.

There's too much pressure.

I sit on the edge of the bed and sit on my hands before I can explode into a racing ball of nerves.

But still, my heart rockets into my throat the second I hear the water in the shower shut off. My ears are simply too powerful, and I hear every movement and can nearly exactly picture every step he takes. As he towels off. As he pulls on the clothes.

And when his hand goes to the doorknob. When he twists it.

And then when he steps out, into our bedroom.

He wears the black pants I grabbed, and I see the waistband of his gray underwear. His feet are bare. He pulls the pale green button up onto his frame, but as his eyes lock with mine, he seems to forget to button it up.

I sit there, frozen. I can only stare at him, so many warring emotions raging through me.

So I focus on him. On his green eyes. On that wild, untamed dark hair. On his lips. On the valley that cuts between his chest muscles and continues in a line down his stomach.

He's so beautiful.

But I quiver inside. I'm a scared mess.

"I don't know where to start," I confess. "After every-thing...all of this. So much has happened. I just..." I shake my head. "I don't even know where to begin."

Cyrus takes a step forward, and another. He comes to stand just before me and reaches out to take one of my hands.

"Are you scared?" he asks gently. He studies my hand, my knuckles.

I nod. "Yes."

His eyes rise up to mine. He doesn't say anything for a moment, as if evaluating my response, and how to give his own. He just keeps looking at me. Reading my soul. Searching down deep.

"I need you to know," he says. And with his first words, I feel this...surge. Pulling me to him. Lacing us together even tighter. "That I have been scared, too. So scared for these past few weeks. The uncertainty. The worry."

I understand. Because I sent him here, back to Roter Himmel, and refused to go with him. I asked for space. For time.

"I understood the pain I've caused you," he says. I look into his eyes, and his voice thickens. He's pale. I can see it: he's still scared. "And finally, I accepted my own."

He kneels so that he is between my legs. He looks up into my face, and I see him. A man submitting. Opening. After 286 years of being alone and ruling with an iron fist, he lays himself vulnerable.

"I need you to know," he says, his voice low and husky. "Before your Resurrection, I watched you, Logan. I saw you. Every move you made. I listened to every breath you took. I was utterly aware of everything you did."

He shifts just slightly closer and my eyes widen and my heart skips a little beat.

He places a hand on my thigh, and his look deepens.

"Everything you did over that month we spent together pushed me further and further. It all slowly drove me mad." I think I see anger gather in his eyes. "At night, dreams of you filled my head, Logan."

My heart flutters, something quivers in my stomach. "The things that wandered through my brain..." he trails off and his voice sounds shamed. "The desires that woke my body up." He shakes his head, but he does not look away.

He reaches forward and caresses my jaw. "I could not admit it to you then, and I could not admit it to myself until just now." He stops for a moment. And I see it. This is hard for him. This is stripping away every ounce of pride he has to say the words. "I fell in love with you over that month, Logan Pierce."

My insides explode into a million diamonds at his confession.

"The hatred I felt toward myself was immeasurable," he continues. "And I hated you. Because in all these centuries, millennia, I never, ever once was tempted by another. I longed for my wife and had never looked at another woman. But then there was you. And for the first time, I lusted for someone I did not *know* was Sevan. I craved your company like every living creature on this earth craves oxygen."

I feel emotion prick the backs of my eyes, and emotion fills Cyrus' own.

I reach up, clasping a hand around Cyrus' wrist. It's hard to breathe. He's filled me to the brim with emotions.

"You said you'd wanted me to love you as you, as Logan," Cyrus breathes. "I hated that I did. I tried not to. But everything, *everything*, about you made me."

He leans in closer, and we breathe the same air. "I am so eternally grateful that we have finally been returned to one another, Sevan. But I also must confess. That for the first time, I fell in love with another."

I lean forward, touching my forehead to his. And my blood goes electric with the connection.

"I did fall in love with you," Cyrus breathes, his breath warming my face. "I am in love with you, Logan."

Every broken piece in me slips into place. All my bitterness and all my hurt. All the injustices I've felt over my twenty years of life slip into a smooth and blissful mirror that reflects the whole me.

I wrap my hand behind his neck, and I can't wait another second longer when I close the distance between our lips.

Our kiss starts out as passionately gentle. Love and acceptance creep into every crevice of it. Admission and progress make it sweet and perfect.

The hunger grows in me. I clasp him harder to me. My lips part and greedily I taste him.

I pull at Cyrus, twisting. He lays back on the bed, and with lust in my eyes, I straddle his hips. My hand caresses his jaw, and I press my chest into his.

Cyrus' hands come to my hips, and electricity sparks its way from my stomach down my legs. His hands are hot and strong, so very, very real.

My hair cascades down around our faces, deepening the darkness.

But my lips move with Cyrus' and our souls melt into one.

That tiny spark of fear creeps up inside of me again though as Cyrus' right hand slips down my hip, onto my bare thigh.

I must have made some small sound. Or maybe he felt my hesitancy.

But Cyrus pulls his lips away from mine. He reaches up and pushes my hair back, tucking it behind my ear, and holds me so gently.

"No one can understand," Cyrus says gently. "How complicated this is. It's difficult, even for me. Because for the first time in my life, I find myself in love with two women."

No wonder it was so hard for Cyrus to admit it, the fact that he loves and loved Logan. Because that part of me, Sevan, the words are difficult for even her to hear.

"I feel I must do right by you, Logan," he says, staring into my eyes. "Because even though I know without a doubt in me that I love you, we still have only spent a month together. I..." he hesitates, and it's obvious he doesn't know how to word this. How this is so complicated.

"We need some time to get to know each other," I fill in for him, the first words I've spoken in a while. "I'm *here*, Cyrus. I am with you. But I do need time."

He studies me, and I see the relief in his face. The echo of what I've just spoken.

"Sevan knows everything about you, and you, everything about her," I say, speaking with the words of both women. "But Logan needs time. I'm still only twenty-years-old. I've still never really had a serious relationship. I've never been married. I've…" I hesitate at the confession, slightly embarrassed, but at the same time, I'm relieved. "I've never even had sex."

Cyrus reaches up again, tucking my hair behind my ear. His eyes are so soft, so open. And I know there's no getting out of this hole. There's no escaping the well I've fallen down into.

"I'm here with you, Cyrus," I say, leaning in closer, his scent filling my nose. "I'll never leave. But I, Logan, need to play this out. I need it to build, in a way that is real to *me*."

Cyrus nods, a little smile pulling on his lips. "Yes," he says. "Anything, Logan."

Logan.

Oh. When he says my name…

He fractures me and pieces me back together all in two syllables.

"But I want you to know this," I say gently, coming closer. "Forgetting every past life, forgetting the first, I, Logan Pierce, have fallen irrevocably in love with a man the world fears and obeys, because I see the real you. Because you take my acid. I love you, Cyrus."

I see what my words do to him. I hear his heart skip. I feel the blood rush through his body. I see his eyes widen just slightly. And I know that the words that come out of his mouth next will be the absolute truth.

"And I, after only this short amount of time," he says, reaching up and cupping a hand behind my neck. "Found a mate who matches my own dark soul. I love you, Logan Pierce."

He means it. I know it, with every doubtful, bitter part of Logan, I know it.

I feel it when he pulls my lips to his.

I feel it as he holds me to him.

I feel his promise to never let me go.

CHAPTER 17

I'VE NEVER SPENT HOURS KISSING ANYONE, BUT THEY PASS quickly wrapped in Cyrus' arms.

He takes things slow. It seems to be enough for him, the touches and our lips fusing together as one. He never pressures me for anything more. And Sevan stays in the back of my head, quiet and dark.

Together, just Logan and Cyrus, we have a perfect day.

But as the night begins to fall outside, I feel the call. The hunger.

Together, Cyrus and I leave the castle. We slip across the valley. And then with incredible speed, we race through the canyon, to where we know the next town is.

It's incredibly easy. There are only a hundred or so humans that live in this little village. But silently, we break into a home, and we drink.

The woman's eyes flash open for just a moment, but paralyzed by my toxins, they slip closed once more.

I suck and pull, looking at Cyrus, who drinks from the man lying beside this woman in bed.

We drink our fill, and when we are full and when I can feel the amount I've taken from her, we leave them be, sleeping it off in their beds, to only awake thinking they've had a nightmare.

Together, we make our way back to the castle, avoiding the encampment of the army that holds the people of the town captive.

Walking through the doors of the castle in the dead of night, my thirst is sated, but my stomach growls with hunger.

"Come on," I say, reaching for Cyrus' hand with a smile. "I'm starving. I'll make us some dinner."

"I thought you couldn't cook?" he questions with a smirk and the upward tilt of his eyebrow.

I shrug. "It's a day for miracles."

I'm sure Cyrus has never been in this kitchen in its current form. It's huge and gleaming with stainless steel. Every gadget possible is tucked here and there, organized to obsession. A huge walk-in refrigerator and freezer sit side by side.

Thoughtfully, I gather ingredients, and I realize, they're all going to go bad within a week with all the help locked up. Better get to cooking.

Together, Cyrus and I make fettuccini Alfredo. When we're finished, we slip into the room next to the kitchen. It's the workers' dining room. There's a roughly hewn wooden table, massively long. It could probably seat twenty people.

But just us, Cyrus and I sit, looking at each other from

across the table as we eat the meal that I only burned a little bit.

"You have to have a lot of questions about what's going on outside," I say, swallowing a bite.

Instantly, Cyrus' eyes darken and his relaxed demeanor falls.

My Logan-esque hardness forms, prepared to have to defend my decisions and actions. And I'm grateful for Sevan there, at my side, who is so confident that this is the right move.

"There are rumors and conformations manifested that Born and Royals alike are trying to take us out," I say. "There were those who came after us—me, in Greendale. They were going to use me to make you step away from the throne. They told me that there was insurrection brewing in Court. And then there was what happened to you."

My eyes slide down to his neck. There isn't even a scar now, but I'll never forget the bloody sight of his head detached from the rest of his body.

"I interrogated the man who did it," I move on. "He snuck over the border. Considering no one sounded the alarm, that he got into the castle silently, I have to think at least one Royal was helping him. And he said something about having no choice but to trust a Royal, if he wanted change."

Cyrus grits his teeth hard, but doesn't say anything.

"I'm trying to take care of this, but there are so few I trust. Larkin is on assignment. But that only leaves me with Alivia, Ian, and Eshan."

At the mention of Alivia's name, Cyrus' eyes flare just a little.

"Yes," I say, sounding annoyed. "She's here. She's helping me. Get over it."

He gives me a little glare, so I immediately move on.

"The man is dead now, but he confessed that there were five others in Roter Himmel who were in on this, too. Two are dead already. But as for any of the Royals who were in on it..." I take another bite, slowly chewing, as everything overwhelms me once more. "We did an initial interrogation and ended up with six I intended to question further."

Cyrus watches me, listening. But he seems uneasy.

"But I knew it wasn't near enough. People can be two-faced liars. So I took a page out of your book." I look up at him, and at my words, his eyes widen a bit. "I needed to make them afraid for their very lives."

"All that out there is staged," Cyrus concludes.

I nod.

"Dorian and Malachi helped me orchestrate it all," I continue. "They loaned me their private human armies and we made them look like the Austrian government. They've all been placed under arrest for killing humans over the years."

"They are going to interrogate Court and try to get them to confess what we are," Cyrus says, sitting back, observing me. I see a twinkle of pride and admiration in his eyes.

I nod. "Anyone who confesses to being a vampire will be shipped off to the Houses around the world, where they can deal with them. They'll never be allowed back at Court. And they'll get a hard, life-long lesson in appreciation for what they had here in Court."

Cyrus nods, but there's still that far away look in his eyes.

"In the end, Court will be severely downsized, but any traitors will be rooted out because they will fear for their lives."

I study Cyrus, now that he's been brought up to speed. He studies the wall behind me, his eyes a bit glazed over.

"These are going to be some dark, tumultuous days in the weeks to come," I say, my voice low and soft. "But in the end, we need to know who we can and cannot trust. Above all, we have to protect our secret."

His eyes slide back over to me when I speak the words he's repeated hundreds of times over the years.

"It's remarkable," he says. But his voice is hollow. "You've done well."

I'm trying to read him, because I know it's there under the surface. But he doesn't say anything more.

Finished eating, I slide my plate away from me.

"Come on," I say as I stand. "Let's go somewhere."

Thirty minutes later, we're both dressed and ready for a day out. Down through the belly of the castle we drop and finally walk out into a huge, cavernous garage. There are dozens of vehicles inside, all in varying degrees of expense and color.

"Think you remember those driving lessons?" I tease him as he opens the door to a very aggressive looking black sports car for me.

"I think I'll manage," Cyrus says, giving me a coy smile. He slips into the driver's seat and the engine purrs to life.

He looks over at me, giving a smirk, and guns the gas.

We rocket through the tunnel that cuts under the castle, and suddenly shoot out into the brilliant sun, with our sunshades securely in place.

It's a trick, navigating through town in the most inconspicuous way. We go down side roads, and even drive over the uneven grass, all to skirt as far around the invaded village as we can. But eventually, we hit the main road at the far side of the lake, and head for the canyon.

It's nearly a two-hour drive from Roter Himmel to the next major town. There are still questions I want to ask, like if Cyrus really was dead during the last week, or if it was just more of a hibernation. But the mood is light. The sun is shining. And Cyrus is holding my hand with the top down on the car.

So I just smile and squeal as he punches the gas.

Cyrus easily navigates us to the center of the city and parks along the curb, putting money in the meter.

"Remind me what we're doing here?" Cyrus asks as I take his hand, tugging him down the sidewalk and toward the first shops. "Out among humans when we've just gone through everything we've been through?"

I look over my shoulder at him, glaring. "We're here exactly because of everything we've been through lately, Cyrus. I've been holding an entire kingdom together, planning a coup, on my own, while you took a damn long nap. A girl needs a little break every now and then."

He smiles, and oh my hell, it's just so damn beautiful. I just have to stop right in my tracks, put my hand on his cheek, and kiss him until we get glares from an old woman walking past us.

I'm feeling like myself—Logan—again. I know it when the salty curse words start slipping out my lips and through my mind.

"Come on," I say, stepping away from Cyrus and pulling him toward a boutique shop.

Cyrus follows closely behind me as I sort through each rack. His hand darts out every now and then, just resting on my hip, or he tucks himself behind me, hugging me tight to his front, and presses his lips to the back of my neck.

I'm such a teenager today.

Because all I can do is smile, occasionally a silly little giggle slips past my lips. I reach up, cupping my hand behind his neck, and pull his lips down to my own.

"How about this?" Cyrus says at one shop, one of dozens.

He grabs a scanty little bikini from off the rack, dangling it temptingly in front of me with a lustful gleam in his eyes.

I give an approving *hmm*, raising an eyebrow at him. "I don't think there's anything quite like this in our closet."

He gives me an approving smile as I put the scanty swimsuit into my bag, along with the other items.

I really wasn't planning on buying this much. There were a few things for me in the closet at the castle. I could have gotten by with just a few additions.

But Cyrus keeps encouraging me to buy anything I look at for more than two seconds. With each shop we go to, his arms get loaded with more and more shopping bags.

He just looks so damn happy though.

"Are you trying to spoil me totally rotten?" I ask when

we step out of another shop, another two bags added to the collection.

"After everything you've endured, you deserve to be pampered," he says with a gleam in his eye. "You've faced identity theft, robbery, a money shark, and horrible ramifications from him in the last short span of your life, Logan." He steps closer, looking down at me with intense eyes. "Let me spoil you."

I can't help but smile, rising up onto my toes, and pressing my lips to his.

The reminder of the sad story that is my luck in my human life flashes something else into my brain.

"Oh!" I declare, my hand darting into my back pocket for my phone. "We promised Amelia pictures of our time in Austria. Come here!" I grab Cyrus by the front of his shirt, pulling him into me.

Extending my arm with the camera turned to us, I snap a picture of our smiling faces. And then I turn my face to his, and as his lips immediately find mine, I snap another.

"I have a feeling we'll be finding a house outside of Roter Himmel at some point so that we can invite your friend for a visit," Cyrus says as he watches me text the pictures to Amelia. "I think she's going to be incredibly disappointed when you don't return home after your year studying abroad."

"Or we can always make a trip back to visit," I say with a smile. Once more I take Cyrus' hand, dragging him down the street, back to our car.

We ditch the shopping bags, and spotting a fancy restaurant across the street, I pull Cyrus along with me.

We spend the entire day in the city. We probably drop over a thousand euros. It's more money than I would have spent on myself in five years back in Greendale.

But when I see how happy Cyrus looks to be doing this, I know this shopping spree was more for him than it was for me.

This is about bonding. Connecting. It's about being normal.

It's getting dark when we get back in the car and Cyrus points us back in the direction of Roter Himmel.

I lean my head back on the headrest, watching the beautiful scenery go by as we roll down the road.

Cyrus holds my hand as we weave through the canyon. The road grows narrower, abandoned.

When we crest the mountain, he slows.

Lanterns dot the land before us. Vaguely I can see the homes and buildings. Mostly the tents set up all over the place. And above it all, looms our home. The castle.

Cyrus drives once more. But there is a fork, where the road splits to the left to return to home, Cyrus turns right, onto a dirt road that looks as if it hasn't been traveled in a while.

"Where are we going?" I ask.

"It's a surprise," he says gently, but there's an excited gleam in his eye.

The road hugs the mountain tightly. Potholes threaten to bottom us out here and there, but Cyrus goes slow, navigating the rough terrain. At one point, for at least a mile, we're sandwiched between the mountainside, and the lake. If we veer slightly left or right, we'd flip, or end up in the water.

The trees grow thick around us, and finally, Cyrus loops the car around a lagoon that settles into the side of the mountain, parking the car on a patch of grass.

There's a gleam of mischief in his eye as he climbs out into the dark night.

I hop out, and watch with a raised eyebrow as he digs through the bags in the trunk. He comes up, holding the swimsuit he bought for himself, and the bikini.

"Care for a dip?"

I laugh at the ridiculous smile on his face and the suggestion. I feel myself blush, but I bite my lower lip, nodding.

I snatch the small bits of fabric from his hand, and tromp off into the trees.

The night is still very warm. Even though we're up in the mountains, it is mid-August. The last surge of summer. I don't even get goosebumps when I step out from the trees, in only the tiny swimsuit that barely covers my boobs and definitely was made to show off this much of my ass.

But I feel myself flush when I spot Cyrus crouched in a tree just at the water's edge. No shirt, in the moonlight, it's a spectacular view. And that look in his eye could melt me clean through the middle of the earth.

"By the god of the moon, you will be the death of me, woman," he breathes, shaking his head with a lustful gaze.

I smile, blushing.

With an elegant leap, Cyrus launches himself into the air, bending in a perfect arc, before cannonballing into the water.

I scream, skirting away from the water's edge when the water splashes.

Cyrus surfaces, flicking his wet hair out of his face. He wears a broad smile. "Come on!"

I go to the water's edge where the grassy land drops down into the water. Carefully, I stretch one leg down, dipping my toe in the water.

"It's freezing!" I protest.

"You're an immortal vampire capable of ripping the face clean off of the best soldier, and you're afraid of a little cold water?" he taunts me. With a wicked glint in his eye, he sends a wave of water splashing in my direction.

"Oh, you are so dead now!" I scream. I take three steps back, before running and launching myself into the air. With a wicked laugh, I splash into the water, right beside Cyrus.

When I surface, I reach up, placing both of my hands on top of his head, and shove him down under the water. He grabs me around the waist as he sinks, and drags me down with him.

Down here in the water, it's dark. But the moon cuts through the rippling surface, making everything look mystical and magical.

Face to face, I look at Cyrus through the water.

His hair floats around him and his skin glows an eerie blue.

He looks supernatural.

I reach out, putting a hand behind his neck. I pull myself to him, our skin feeling cold in the water when it connects.

Slowly, we rise to the surface, and water trails down our faces.

But I stare at him in the moon. His eyes. That strong nose. And those lips.

"I've never seen lips I love more than yours," I confess without even thinking. But instead of feeling embarrassed, I brush my thumb over them. They part, breathing warm air on my own lips.

Cyrus' hands come to my hips, pulling me in close. I raise my legs in the water, wrapping them around his waist.

I feel so alive.

So electric.

So present.

"Kiss me," I command.

Cyrus happily obliges.

He sucks my soul from me, stealing it. Claiming it as his own. And I draw in his. I feel him, filling every part of me, until I can't identify what parts are me and what parts are him.

I cling to Cyrus, letting him run his hands over me. I grip his bare skin greedily, hungry for more, but filled to the brim.

I never want this day to end. It's been perfect. Normal. And I can feel it. It's just me and Cyrus here. Just Logan. None of this day has Cyrus been reaching for Sevan. He hasn't kissed her once this day.

Cyrus is mine.

CHAPTER 18

WE'RE BOTH SOPPING WET WHEN A FEW HOURS LATER WE head back to the castle. Neither of us brought a towel considering our swimming venture was spur of the moment. I hope Cyrus' nice car isn't totally ruined considering how much lake water we're getting everywhere.

Back to the castle we go, and together, we unload the shopping bags, still only each wearing our swimming suits.

"We're going to have to hire a new maid, just to handle all of this," Cyrus teases as we climb the stairs to our bedroom.

"Don't you try to put this on me," I scold him, shooting a withering stare at him over my shoulder. "Who kept adding every single thing to the shopping bag?"

He only laughs and follows me into the bedroom.

I've just set them down in our closet, when my phone dings from inside one of them. I hunt through the plastic and fabric until I find it.

Amelia: *OMG!!! You two are just to die for! Shopping AND kissing in Europe?? It can't get much better than that!*

I smile, beginning to reply, when another text comes through. *Your dad has to be getting more on board with you and Collin now. How could he not see how happy you are?*

A block of ice drops in my stomach, instantly melts, and sends ice cold acid rushing through all of my veins.

I feel sick.

My ears are ringing.

"Logan?" Cyrus questions from out in the bedroom.

Numbly, my eyes rise to meet his.

"Logan, what's wrong?" he asks, taking two steps forward.

I shake my head. The ringing in my ears is loud. So loud. And I swear I've turned into a block of dry ice.

I take two steps out of the closet, but my eyes once more fall to my phone.

Your dad... Your dad... Your dad...

The words scream at me over and over and over.

She doesn't know.

"Logan?" Cyrus says once more.

"The day the intruder beheaded you," I say. And I hate those words, but even more, I hate the ones I have to confess in just a second. "I'd just been back at my parents' house in Greendale." I dim the screen, hugging the phone to my chest. "Cyrus, the men who came after me, they killed my parents. Tortured them. I've seen some gruesome things at the mortuary, but nothing like what they put my parents through."

"Logan," Cyrus says, stepping forward and pulling me into his arms. "I had no idea. I'm...I'm so sorry."

Numbly, I lay my head on his cool chest. "I left Larkin behind to take care of things, make sure there was no evidence. Just a few nights ago, Eshan and I buried them in the courtyard graveyard."

"Eshan is here?" Cyrus asks in surprise.

I nod. "He's staying," I say with finality, even though I know Cyrus won't fight me about it. "With my parents gone, there's no one to take care of him. And with what he knows now…" I shake my head, realizing one more fact Cyrus doesn't know. "He spent four days as a Bitten."

And I get a little scared, because I remember Cyrus' reaction when once a few months ago we had a conversation about them. How angry he was. How he forbid Elle from using the Bitten cure anymore.

But Cyrus only looks down at me with sympathy on his face.

Emotion wells in my eyes as everything hits me again.

I'm so tired.

I've been through these things, all this drama, over and over.

"It's too much," Cyrus says. His words come out clear and confident. "We have dealt with all of this over and over. We have handled the problems of our kind for thousands of years." He shakes his head. I see a darkness creep into his eyes. "It is our turn for peace now."

My brows furrow as I look up into his dark eyes. "What do you mean?"

Cyrus shakes his head again. "It is already happening, Sevan. The kingdom is crumbling and our system is shaken."

He takes my hands in his, holding them to his chest. "Sevan, after all this time, I am tired. Let…let us be done with it all."

Confusion sinks into my expression and my mouth opens, but no words come out at first. I take half a step back to get a better view of his face. He's serious.

"You…you just want to walk away?" I ask. "Abandon Court and the Houses and just…let them figure all this crap out?"

Still, his face darkens, but I read all the sincerity there. He's sure about this. "We have done everything for them. There are others, every House leader can help begin a new system. Over and over we have solved their problems, and all we have to show for it is a world that thinks I am a violent mad man!"

Cyrus takes a step away from me, turning to the window. He braces his hands on the windowsill, looking out over the valley and those he speaks about.

"I am tired, Sevan," he says. He stays like that for a very long minute, just watching them. Then slowly, he stands. He turns back to me. He crosses the room until he's standing right in front of me. He raises a hand, cupping his palm gently to my cheek.

"After all this time, I have come to the realization that the only thing I care about, the only thing I've truly cared about for a long while, is you." He says the words softly. So gently. "I am done with the rest of the world. From now on, my only concern is enjoying every second I have with you, and finding a way to break the curse that takes you away from me."

I'm frozen. I can only stare at Cyrus in wonder while my heart goes insane.

Everything Cyrus has created is incredible. An entire new race. The politics we operate by. The governance of twenty-seven Houses spread throughout the world, and everything there is here at Court.

He's ready to walk away from it all.

He's ready to drop the crown.

So we can be together. Just the two of us. For once.

I let my eyes slide closed, and for just a second I relish in that love. I take hold of it, gathering it into my chest, and appreciate the size of it.

I want that. More than anything.

"No," I say evenly.

I let my eyes slide back open. They meet Cyrus', and I see in them just how much he disagrees with my one, single word.

"We started all of this," I say, taking his hands in mine and holding them to my chest. "All of that out there, all of them spread throughout the world, they exist because of us, because of choices we made a long time ago. They are our family. If we just walk away…"

I shake my head, looking at my husband with wide eyes.

"I can't do that," I say. I swallow once, because my throat feels thick and dry. "Yes, there are those who are betraying us. But most of them… They're innocent. They're just living their lives, the ones we constructed so they can have peace. Most of them are not prepared for what would happen if we walked away."

Cyrus opens his mouth to speak, but I push on, cutting him off.

"Imagine it, Cyrus," I beg him, pleading with my eyes. "If we disappeared, if they no longer feared you. What would the world become? Because our son was far from the only one of our kind who thought we shouldn't have to hide. Those who thought like that would gather in weeks. In months they'd form armies. They'd turn against the humans. And maybe they would stand a chance at gaining power and domination, but there are so many humans." I shake my head. I'm filled to the brim with fear as I imagine it. "If they all united to hunt us down, we would be eradicated within a few short years. And then everything you created, after all the sacrifice, it would all have been for nothing."

In his eyes, I can see that I am not winning. I'm not swaying him.

"It wouldn't be for nothing," Cyrus says. His voice is hard, strained. "Because instead of perhaps sixty years together, we have had lifetimes. There has been pain and separation, yes. But all these years." His eyes are hard as he looks down at me. "It would not have been for nothing."

Once more his eyes harden.

He turns, and he walks toward the doors. "I am tired, Sevan. After all this time, I'm tired."

He pulls the door open.

"Then I will carry you for a while," I say, feeling like I'm fracturing into a dozen sharp pieces.

Cyrus stalls, looking back at me. I can't quite tell what he's thinking. But he turns back to the door, and walks out.

Stab, stab, stab.

It feels like I'm hit with a thousand little darts. Pricked over and over by the pain of disagreement. But understanding.

Because I'm tired, too.

I want to run away together, to just live a simple, normal life with the man I love.

But now is not the time.

You have to understand, I tell myself. *You have no idea what he's just been through. Give him time to adjust.*

So I make a deal with myself. Take a breath, give Cyrus some space. And keep doing what I've been doing since I arrived in Roter Himmel.

CHAPTER 19

FOR TWO DAYS, I GIVE CYRUS HIS SPACE. I DON'T necessarily avoid him, but I wait for him to seek me out. Which he doesn't.

So on the sixth day since the invasion of the army, I slip out of the castle during the day. I pull on my darkest sunshades, and I sneak down to the same house I slipped out of before, the headquarters of this plot.

A guard immediately sticks a gun in my face, demanding to know how I escaped lock up. But Matthias Reiter steps into the building, dismissing the man.

"I am impressed with your ability to stay so removed," he says in an unidentifiable accent. "With all that is going on."

"I've been otherwise occupied," I say, absolutely zero patience right now.

"Leave her be, Matthias," a voice says from the dark. From the hallway steps Malachi. He glares at the general with dark eyes. Matthias doesn't seem intimidated, but he does head back in the direction he came from.

"Where is Dorian?" I ask, looking around to see if he's hiding in the shadows, too.

"He is assisting with the interrogations," Malachi explains, walking over to the window. It's covered with heavy shutters, but he sets sunshades on his face, and opens them to look out.

"Have we identified any traitors yet?" I ask, going to stand beside him.

Looking out, I see how they have handled keeping a town full of vampires captive.

Guards stand outside of every building. They're keeping the vampires inside, away from the painful sun. They keep them from escaping with their weapons.

"So far three individuals have admitted to being vampires," Malachi says with a sigh. "Most are staying strong. They maintain that they do not know that their former leader is anything other than human."

I nod. I want to get through all of this now. It's impossible to be patient with so much on the line.

"This is going to take some time," he says, as if he can read my thoughts.

I sigh. This is going to be the difficult part in all of this for me. These immortals have lived such long lives, what is a couple weeks or months to them?

But it's forever to me as Logan. It's forever when I know my brother is tied up in all of this. When Alivia and Ian are stuck in the thick of it all and I know they're innocent.

I'll extract them at some point. Let them in on everything. Alivia needs to return to her house, and soon.

But I have to let them all believe this is real. It's about fooling those who are watching them.

"Are you sure you want to do this, my Queen?" Malachi asks. "They all fully believe you're in captivity. There's no need to prove anything."

I nod, steeling my gaze. "I have to. I can't let there be any hint of doubt that this is real."

Malachi nods, a look of deepening sadness in his eyes, and reverent respect.

He nods, and Matthias steps back out. Without hesitating, which makes me believe that he's enjoying this, he snaps handcuffs around my wrists, which is laughable. I could break them easily.

But I couldn't survive the assault rifle that he places at my back, over my heart, and the pain I'm about to experience when he pulls my sunshades off is very real.

"After you," he says with a smile in his voice. He reaches forward, flinging the door open, and pushes me out into the sun with the tip of his gun.

A cry of pain leaps from my lips as I step out into the brilliant sun. I'm blind, everything a glow of white. It's like ten knives are stabbed into each eyeball, and they're all white-hot.

Through town, I walk with the gun pressed to my back. I make sure to scream plenty, but I also try to make it seem like I'm attempting to be tough. I try to act like I am a queen and that I'm being strong for my people.

So much fake.

So many faces I have to wear.

But it will all be worth it in the end.

Matthias guides me to The Communal. It's a hotel with a bar on the main floor. It's old. It's been a center for Roter Himmel for hundreds of years. A gathering place for Royals who travel here, a right of passage to some degree. It's a place where others congregate, to drink and socialize.

Of course it would be where they're holding many of the Royals.

"You've found nothing," I growl at Matthias as he marches me up the stairs to the building. "Take your men and leave."

"Not until you give us the answers I want," he counters, clearly enjoying our little ruse.

I stumble through the door when he shoves me with the barrel of his gun. But I sigh, relieved that it's dimmer inside.

Dimmer, but only marginally.

A short hallway immediately opens up to the lounge. There's a bar against the far wall and tables and chairs are scattered throughout the large space. Other rooms break off down hallways. There's a staircase that goes up from next to the bar, and upstairs, I know there are rooms for guests.

But all the windows are open. They let in the brilliant summer light, and my head still throbs.

"Take a seat," Matthias says loudly and with bite to his tone. He shoves me to a table in the center of the room and I sink into it, glaring up at the man.

We're being loud. We're doing this in a public place. Because we want every part of this conversation to be overheard.

"I'm not saying a word until you close those shutters," I snarl. "I can't even think straight and you expect me to give you honest and true answers in an interrogation?"

"And why do you need the shutters closed, Ms. Sevan?" Matthias asks, laying his hands flat on the table and leaning in toward me.

"I've got a migraine," I say, narrowing my eyes and leaning toward the man.

It really is too easy. I've got all this acid in me, and Matthias doesn't have to fake much. He really is a nasty boss man.

It's almost fun.

"You're a difficult one to peg down," Matthias finally says, standing and going to one set of shutters. He closes one, looks over at me, waits dramatically, and closes the other.

Real relief sighs through me though as the room becomes darker.

The searing pain in my eyes lessens just a bit.

"It's obvious you're someone important to these people," he says as he continues going around the room and closing shutters. "The way they talk about you, you being in that castle. It appears you've recently returned. From where, I haven't yet puzzled that out. But these people, they do seem to love you."

"I take care of them," I say. "Loyalty goes both directions."

Matthias closes the last shutter as four more guards step into the room, each wielding a deadly-looking firearm.

"And what about the man some have called the King?" Matthias questions. Slowly, he walks back to me, and he stands at one corner of the table, looking down at me. "I get the impression that they meant to keep him off their lips, but more than one has slipped. The great country of Austria has no king and hasn't for over one hundred years. So tell me, where is this King and when can I speak to him?"

I feel little barbs bristle all over me. I don't want to pretend that Cyrus is dead. Not when for a week and a half I wasn't sure if he was or not. I want to scream it out for the entire world to hear, that Cyrus is alive.

But now is not the time.

"He's dead," I say, letting my eyes drop to the tabletop. "Someone murdered him a week ago."

"My condolences on the loss of your husband." He says it in a way that is supposed to reveal that he's figured this fact out, that this King is the other half to my Queen. "But tell me, Sevan. Why would they call him King?"

My eyes rise up to meet his. This really is too easy to fake.

Roter Himmel has been strong. We've been left alone for a very long time. But there has always been fear in the back of my mind. Fear of a situation exactly like this one, that someday we would be discovered and investigated, and I would have to answer questions just like these.

"Words are just words," I say. "The people could call him a monkey or a vegetable and he would still only be a man."

Matthias smiles, and I wonder: how did he come to be a part of this? When did he learn about our kind, and when did Dorian decide he was trustworthy?

But if Dorian trusts him in this, I trust him.

"You say you have a migraine," he moves along. "It

makes me wonder if there is something wrong with the very air here. I've heard that excuse a hundred times in the last two days. But surely that is illogical."

"It's been a stressful couple of days," I say. "We're all having a bad week."

"I've never seen group migraines, Sevan," he says, sitting down in the chair across from me. "I've never seen a migraine so severe that it caused anyone to scream like that at the exposure of sunlight. I've never seen a migraine make eyes turn so bloodshot it was as if they were bleeding from within. I've never seen a migraine instill so much fear at the prospect of being taken out into the sun."

I just stare at Matthias. I don't have any words right now, and I don't really need them.

"Tell me, Sevan," he says, leaning forward and folding his arms on the table. "Why, after some repeated exposures in the sun, have no less than seven of the members of this peculiar little town, confessed to being vampires?"

I already knew this was a fact. Well, Malachi told me that three had confessed. But even though I was already warned, it still hits me like a slap across the face.

I feel betrayed.

There's a little spike of fear that jumps up in the pit of my stomach that worries over what Cyrus will do to those who betrayed our secret.

I force myself to chuckle. I smile, and tilt my head to the side just a little. "And you believe them?" I pause, staring Matthias down. "Vampires aren't real."

I believe every inch of that evil looking smile that curls on his lips. He's so good at this.

"Thank you for your time," he says, suddenly standing. "We'll speak again, very soon, when you're feeling more truthful and cooperative. Until then, I hope you feel like deepening your tan. You're looking a little pale."

"No," I say, putting a trace of fear in my voice. "No, I…" But I trail off.

And it has the immediate desired effect.

"Sevan!" someone yells from inside the building.

"She's just a woman!" another person calls from inside. "Let her go!"

"Please, let us go!" someone else cries.

It takes every ounce of self-control I have not to look over at Matthias and give a conspiratorial smile. But there's always the chance we are being watched.

Roughly, he drags me to my feet and hauls me out to the doors. I take a deep breath and squeeze my eyes closed against the burning sunlight, and I scream. Then there is the sound of bodies pounding on walls. There's screams and I hear my name shouted over and over. Others yell at the guards and I hear furniture being smashed to the ground as a riot breaks out.

There's a gunshot that echoes deafeningly through the entire town.

I whip back, prepared to run inside. But Matthias is there, pressing a hand into my chest, his eyes serious. "All of my men have been instructed to never shoot to kill unless their lives are in immediate danger," he hisses in a whisper. "You set this up, Sevan, to accomplish something monumental. You have to deal with the fact that there may be repercussions."

My eyes are wild and terrified as I look at him. But as my thundering heart comes to accept his words, I know he's right.

I have to accept it.

And I have to remember, this isn't entirely my fault. I was pushed to this. Because someone else made choices, choices that threatened us all.

This is for the greater good.

I nod once, and turn back to the blindingly brilliant road outside, and march myself in front of Matthias, looking like a good little prisoner.

An hour later, when I get word that the riot has been quieted and no one was killed, I return to the castle, with a dark, heavy heart.

CHAPTER 20

WITH THE SUN SUNK BELOW THE HORIZON HOURS AGO, I can't stand it any longer.

This is enough. Enough with the wallowing in self-pity. Enough acting like a child.

I set off through the castle, straining my ears for the sounds of Cyrus and his whereabouts.

He's not in any of the grand ballrooms. He is nowhere to be found in the lab. The armories are empty. Through each passageway and hall I look.

I'm really, really disturbed when I stumble upon something I've never seen before, tucked way down in the fifth level of the castle. It looks like a club. With private rooms and poles and everything.

I'm going to kill Cyrus for that. He better have some good answers.

But further through the castle I explore.

Each bedroom is empty. He isn't in the kitchen.

For a minute, I start to get scared.

What if something happened to him? What if one of these Born or Royal who betrayed us has found Cyrus yet again and sought his demise once more?

Or what if he truly meant what he said? That he's tired. What if he's…what if he's left?

My stomach feels like a sick, hard knot. Sweat breaks out onto my palms and I stand in a central hallway, turning little circles.

But suddenly, there, in the back of my brain, a dim light bulb flickers on.

There is one more place, somewhere I haven't stepped foot in for over five hundred years. But it's the last possible place.

There is one lone tunnel that branches off of another on the sixth floor. The doorway is hidden, a series of walls that blend together. You would only find the entrance if you knew it was there.

I slip between the walls, and set off through the pitch-black tunnel that burrows straight back, into the deep heart of the mountain.

The path goes on and on for what feels forever. But when light tickles the edges of my vision again, I slow my pace. My feet don't make any sound, and as I see the opening at the end of the tunnel widen, my insides go cold and still.

Ice creeps through every one of my veins. I feel my limbs tighten, as if a black snake slithers around them, constricting. Dread drips into my brain, my eyes, my throat. My stomach.

I can hardly move as I step from the protection of the

tunnel, and into the place that encompasses my worse nightmares.

It's a cave. A cavern. The space opens up fairly wide, probably forty feet across, and sits in a fairly even circle. The floor has been leveled out smooth. But the walls jut up high above me. At least three hundred feet. They sail so high that the ceiling is nearly lost in the dark.

But there, at the crest of the cave, there is a small hole. About three feet in diameter. Moonlight spears into the cave, barely illuminating it.

Cyrus kneels in the center of the cave, staring at the walls. He's utterly still, totally silent.

I want to be sick. I could vomit. There's the sharp taste of metal in the back of my throat. I'm pretty sure all of my cells are slowly transforming into steel. But I take three more steps inside, fully illuminated by the light of the moon.

There are seven crypts that surround us. Gorgeous, intricate openings with arches and platforms along the cave walls.

Resting in each one of them, out in full, plain sight, is a skeleton.

Emotion pricks my eyes as I look around at each one of them.

My throat is so thick it's painful.

I can't breathe.

As if falling back through time, I let my eyes study them one by one.

The body of La'ei.

Edith.

Antoinette.

Shaku.

There rests the body of Helda.

Jafari.

And finally, there in the center, straight across from where I stand, where Cyrus kneels before, are the bones of Sevan.

Tears slip from my eyes as I stare at them.

What is this curse? What is this magic that rips me from body to body, with all my memories, from face to face? What kind of evil saw this as fair?

I feel my mind wanting to fracture as I stand here, seeing all of these skeletons. I remember every detail of living in every one of those bodies. I remember racing across the sand, I remember swimming in the ocean in the moonlight. I remember meals eaten and long journeys taken.

Every one of them lies there, devoid of skin, organ-less. Only stringy hair clings to La'ei and Edith's skeletons. Even the burial clothes on the bodies of the first four have deteriorated with time.

I hug myself, subconsciously checking to make sure that I am alive. That I possess skin, and that my heart beats underneath it.

"Except for the times I have been traveling," Cyrus suddenly speaks up, "I have visited this sepulcher every day since I laid the body of La'ei to rest."

I can't move.

I want to go to his side, to be strong and hold Cyrus in what is surely a deep well of painful memories. But I can't. I'm frozen in place, frozen in this vortex of time.

"Everything in me wishes to go and look for the body of the eighth," he says, emotion ripping at his vocal cords. "But the logical part of me knows there isn't a chance I would ever find Itsuko's remains. And I cannot put into words the amount of grief that brings to my soul, knowing she—you, were alone at the end of that life."

His words are the same as if he had ripped claws across the front of my chest, catching down through bone and all the way to my tender, fleshy heart.

I close my eyes, and clear as day, the memories of all the fear I felt floods through me. The days of anticipation, knowing how they were going to try to use me against Cyrus, they wash over me. And then the bitter realization that I could stop everything.

I remember the rough feel of the whaling spear. The splinter that immediately found its way into my right thumb. For just a fraction of a second, I considered not doing it. But I knew. I knew I would return someday. I knew I had to save my love.

I remember the white-hot cold that ripped through me as I plunged the sharp tip into my chest.

And then the darkness that welcomed me with comforting arms.

Cyrus turns, looking back at me. There's so much pain in his eyes, and I can see the depths of it. I could trip into his eyes and fall for two thousand years before I found the bottom of his grief.

"The happiness in me at your return holds worlds in its weight, *im yndmisht srtov*," he confesses. "But it also fills me with so much fear I feel as if I am drowning. Because the countdown is now initiated for when the end will arrive once more."

I see his face fracture. One tiny crinkle in his face at a time. His eyes squint closed, his lips part.

I'm beside him in an invisible movement. I kneel before him, placing my hands on either side of his face. I press my lips to his forehead, pulling him into my chest.

Great sobs rip from Cyrus, uncontrolled and loud. His hands rise, gripping the back of my shirt in them, clinging to me like his life depends on it.

"I cannot bear it again, Sevan," he sobs. He shakes his head slightly, clinging tighter. "I cannot survive losing you another time."

I splay my hand across the back of his head, pressing his face deeper into my chest. Tears roll down my face as I break, splintered apart by the pain I feel for the man I love more than the world and time and the universe.

I want to whisper promises to him, reassurances.

But I can't.

Not when we know for a fact that my death will happen again.

Not when it's been proven over and over, eight irrefutable times.

"I will always return to you," is all that I can actually promise him. "I will always fight my way back to you, Cyrus."

We cling to one another, sobbing messes filled beyond the brim with pain and loss.

But at least we are here, together.

Some time later, I sit back, looking into Cyrus' face. His skin is spotted with redness, his eyes puffy. Rivers of dried tears stain his cheeks.

But still, I look at him, and he's the most beautiful thing I've ever seen.

I slide a hand down his face, studying him.

"I meant what I said before, Sevan," he says, still holding onto me like his life depends on it. "I don't care about them anymore. I don't care about the throne. All I care about is my time with you, and finding a way to fix this."

His words harden the tender mood we've just created. But he moves on as he reaches up, brushing his thumb over my lips.

"But I understand that you need to see them through," he says. He doesn't look me in the eyes. He studies my face, every little detail. The corners of my eyes, the arch of my lips. "You are the All Mother. They love you, and I understand that you love them. And so I will stay. I will be at your side, but I will not occupy my time trying to save them from what they are too ignorant to understand. But I will stay at your side, Queen Sevan."

I feel it then. As if he had physically taken the crown from his head and placed it upon my own.

The burden and weight of the kingdom will remain on my shoulders, even now that Cyrus has been brought back from the darkness.

But I made him a promise three days ago. That I would carry him.

I will keep that promise.

For however long he needs.

He has carried the burden on his own for centuries while I was dead.

Now it is my turn.

I nod, bringing my face close to his. "Thank you," I manage, and I truly am grateful.

Because if he was truly determined to leave, to walk away from Roter Himmel, I don't know if I would be strong enough to stay with the people, if I could be strong enough *not* to go with him.

I tilt his head toward mine, and press my lips to his.

Things are changing. So much will be different.

But not this.

Not my love for Cyrus.

Not his love for me.

That will never, ever change.

CHAPTER 21

THE VERY NEXT DAY IS THE FIRST THAT WE GET A PHONE CALL to Cyrus' direct office line. I answer, holding my shoulders back.

It took longer than I expected, for word to get out about what happened to Cyrus. It's the House of Martials. They're the first to call and ask if it is true, if Cyrus had been killed.

I assure Elle that no, Cyrus is not dead. He's well and alive and busy working. She asks if Alivia was able to help me identify my father, and I tell her yes. And I'm grateful that she doesn't ask me anything else regarding her brother or sister-in-law. I don't want to have to lie to her.

Another call comes in the next day, also asking about Cyrus' status as living or dead. It's the House of Sidra. They inquire as to why they have not been able to reach anyone at Court.

So I tell them a partial truth. That we are having some internal issues here, that we need to find assurances of trust, and we are currently under lockdown while we sort this out. Any inquiries can come directly to me.

The call from the House of Valdez gets a little heated. They demand to know why they haven't been able to reach their brother and son, Horatio. I explain. And they go off about how I can trust him, how dedicated he is to the crown, how he's been of service to Cyrus for years, enough to be invited to live at Court.

I think I actually believe them when I finally get off the phone.

Over the next few days, our daytime hours are spent separate. Cyrus keeps himself busy in the lab. I handle the flood of inquiries that come in from around the world. Everyone is worried, confused. Rumors have spread around the globe like wildfire.

So over the next few days, I make endless phone calls. One by one, I get in contact with each of the Houses. I assure them that Cyrus is alive and well. No, he has not called them himself because he's the King and is obviously indisposed. Yes, it's true, this is Queen Sevan, the All Mother. Court is currently in lock down. If they have further questions or concerns, they can work directly with me, but obviously I'm incredibly busy dealing with the issues here at Court.

The reactions I'm met with are mixed. Some are doubtful that I am who I say I am. I have to explain that I am the daughter of not one, but two Royals, that my mother is the famed Alivia Conrath, and my father was a member at Court. I give them a fact or two if they tie to the individual House leader, and eventually they accept that I am who I say I am.

Then they turn to reverence and awe. Excitement.

And then they're doubtful again, because they want proof that Cyrus is actually alive. They heard he'd been decapitated, how could he be alive? They think I lie about his wellbeing.

So I get angry.

I channel both my fury as Logan and my commanding ability as Sevan.

I'm not above threatening and vile words.

Each and every phone call is ended with an apology and humbled words.

Good.

I'm so busy that I don't even have time to see what Cyrus is doing down in the lab. But every night, when the sun goes down, I go down to the main floor and find him coming up from the lower levels.

I smile when I see him, and I remind myself that everything is going to be okay when I see the smile that fills his face and spreads to his eyes.

I cross the space, wrapping my fingers into his hair as I press my lips to his.

On the fifth night after visiting the sepulcher, Cyrus and I find ourselves in the watch tower meeting room. I lay on one of the couches, staring up at the chandelier above us, my head in Cyrus' lap.

"Let's go on a trip together," I say, lacing my fingers through his. "Once this is all settled and everything is fixed and we know we're safe, let's take that trip."

Cyrus looks down at me.

Those eyes.

Oh. I love those eyes.

"We could go now," he says, raising an eyebrow.

I glare at him even through the little smile on my face. I roll over, climbing to my knees. I crawl over, placing one knee on either side of his hips, settling into his lap. "Don't even go there," I chide him. But I lace my fingers into his hair, enjoying its thickness, the cool feeling of it between my fingers. His hair is always messed up the last few nights.

I think I've found another favorite thing about him.

"We went on trips as kids," I say, looking down into his eyes. "But we only ever went so far. I always wanted to see the world. And now I want to see it with you."

Cyrus reaches up, tucking hair behind my ear. "Where have you always wanted to go?"

"Somewhere tropical," I say. I study his lips, thinking about all the places in the world I want to kiss them. "With white sandy beaches and water so blue and clear you can see the fish swimming."

"Bora Bora perhaps," Cyrus suggests. "Or maybe even Fiji."

I bite my lower lip, nodding. "And then I want to see penguins."

"Penguins?" he questions with a smile and the raise of an eyebrow.

"Penguins," I confirm with a little laugh. "I know it's colder than Satan's nipples, but I always thought an excursion to Antarctica would be amazing."

"Well then," Cyrus says, shifting and laying me on my back and poising above me. "To Antarctica we will go."

The heat in Cyrus' eyes is intense. It could burn me to my skeleton. But I relish in it. I place a hand on his cheek.

I realize, I can't stop touching his face because I'm still in awe that he's alive. I'm still proving to myself over and over that he's here.

I'll keep touching him for the rest of my life, because I still can't quite believe it.

My lips meet his immediately because I can't stand the separation. Greedily, I pull his lower lip into my mouth, biting it gently. I slide my hands under his shirt, tracing my fingers up and over his stomach muscles.

"You have no idea how badly I wanted to do this back in Colorado," I growl into Cyrus mouth as my hands continue their exploration.

"I know exactly how badly you wanted to do this," he counters as his left hand slips down my hip, rounding my ass, pulling me tight to him. "It's as badly as I wanted my hands on you, Logan. It's as bad as I wanted these here." He squeezes my butt and I smile lustfully. "As badly as I wanted my lips here." He shifts, bringing them to my neck, trailing wet, possessive kisses down my flesh.

Greedily, I pull at his shirt, attempting to remove it, but I rip it clean in half in my haste.

Cyrus' eyes alight red, glowing dim but hot.

And I take him in for a second, being lustful and selfish.

Every pane of his face, every angle of his shoulders and rise and fall of his chest and stomach…

I want this man. Every bit of him. For forever.

I raise up, pushing Cyrus back as I climb on top of him. His hands slip underneath my own shirt, his hands pressed to the bare skin of my back as our lips find each other once more.

There's nothing soft or gentle about these kisses. They're wild and desperate. Hungry and saturated with passion.

But he does not pressure me. He doesn't reach for my zipper. His hands do not wander too far.

He made me a promise, to do this the way I need.

And he's keeping it.

He rolls over, and we slip off the couch. On the ground, he props himself up on an elbow, looking down at me.

I reach up, touching his face, gentle, soft.

"I love you," I say. I feel those three words from my tongue, down to my heels.

He reaches up, brushing his thumb over my lips. "I love you, Logan."

He leans down, kissing me once more.

THE NEXT NIGHT, AFTER ANOTHER EXHAUSTING DAY OF work and politics, Cyrus and I eat together in the kitchen. Cyrus cooked. I fantastically burned the meal I tried to prepare.

"What do you know about Lorenzo?" I ask as I fork the spinach salad.

"Why do you ask?" he says. Then suddenly his gaze flicks up, and he studies my eyes. "Oh," he says, surprise and...guilt flooding into his face. "He's your biological father, isn't he?"

I nod, offering a little smile. He's feeling guilty, because after all this time, he hasn't once asked me about it. "Alivia identified him, and it's pretty obvious. I talked to him, but only for a few minutes."

Cyrus straightens, taking a deep breath. He looks around, as if searching the space for his answers.

"He's not been one of the more memorable members of this Court over the years," Cyrus says. He rubs his hands together, pressing them into his lap. "He's been here at Court for a long time. I'd say, since you were you as Antoinette."

He's old then. At least six hundred years, maybe even seven or eight.

"The man comes and goes. He occasionally attends parties. But he has never been particularly involved in the politics."

"Is there anything concerning about him that you worry about?" I ask, taking another bite.

Cyrus contemplates that for a moment. He shrugs and shakes his head. "Not that I am aware of. For creating what he did, I'd say the man is rather unremarkable."

I give an affirmative noise, but really, I'm just relieved.

Unremarkable is a good thing. It means he likely isn't an evil scumbag.

Thinking of scumbags...

"I've been meaning to ask you," I say, feeling slightly uncomfortable, but also feeling something prickly and hot inflate in my chest. "While I was looking for you last week, I came across something very interesting buried in the fifth floor."

Immediately, Cyrus freezes, his eyes stuck on the plate in front of him.

"How long ago did you open that little blood club in our home, Cyrus?"

I'm really not that mad. I know Cyrus. I know that he

never used it himself.

Really, I'm just enjoying making him squirm.

"Sevan, it was never intended for me," he finally says, looking up at me.

There's so much guilt and shame in his face, it actually makes me laugh. One slips over my lips and a smile cracks my façade.

"The other Court members, we were having a problem with some of the males going after women," he continues stumbling over himself to explain. "I worried about exposure and all the people who would get hurt. This was the solution we came up with."

"And you had to build it within the walls of our home?" I question.

That part really does bother me.

"I only wanted to be sure I could monitor the situation and what happened down there." Oh, it's just comical how mortified and guilty Cyrus looks right now. His eyes are wide, his mouth open, his skin is pale. Poor guy. "I swear to you, I never indulged in the activities that went on inside that club."

A little smile curls in one corner of my mouth. I look up at him from beneath my lashes. "I believe you, Cyrus. I know you would never. But I still want it out of my home. Once we have help in the castle again I want it gone."

"Done," he replies immediately, a slight look of relief in his eyes.

I roll my eyes and shake my head. "Come here, you idiot," I say as I reach across the table, grabbing the front of his shirt. I pull him forward, and kiss him.

CHAPTER 22

THE WILL OF THE BORN IS STRONG, APPARENTLY. FUELED BY their hatred of the crown.

Larkin didn't get much of any information out of the three Born he found. Only vile words about the fall of the crown now that Cyrus was dead. Only that times would change.

Larkin returned to the secure location one day to find two of those Born dead, and the other long gone, with a stash of supplies and a vehicle taken.

I told him he couldn't stop looking for that last Born.

He left to hunt the man down.

Within seven days of my fake interrogation with Matthias, no less than six more Court members confess to being vampires, bringing the total up to thirteen. Thirteen immortals, used to living an easy life at Court, who will be banished from here forever. That is thirteen Houses around the world that will be given a new member to keep an eye on for the rest of their immortal lives.

In the end, we'll be smaller, but we'll be safe.

I've just walked back into the castle from a long afternoon talking with my grandsons when Cyrus steps into the entry, a fat man in some kind of clergy outfit, and an older woman with silver dreadlocks trailing behind her.

I stop in place, eying the strangers warily.

"Cyrus?" I question. My knees bend just slightly, and it's everything I can do to not let my eyes ignite brilliant red, ready to hunt.

"This is Father Patrick and Grace Stevens," Cyrus says, extending his hand in their direction. "They are here at my request."

I raise an eyebrow slightly, still confused and questioning.

Cyrus reaches for my hand, and I can't quite turn my back to the two human strangers as Cyrus guides us through a passageway toward the Great Hall. Neither of them seems bothered by my distrustful behavior.

Cyrus pulls a chair out for me at the huge banquet table. I don't want to sit, but Cyrus seems so relaxed and unconcerned. So I sit, trusting him.

The strangers sit across from us.

"Father Patrick and Grace arrived just this morning at my request," Cyrus begins to explain. "They both have experience with the unexplainable."

My brows furrow and I look at Cyrus. Annoyance creeps up my throat, and it tastes a lot like betrayal.

"I asked them to come here and speak to us about curses," Cyrus says bluntly.

My eyes snap back to the two strangers, and for a moment, there's a painful little surge of hope in my chest.

"My father used to put his hands on my mother when I was a child," Father Patrick says. His voice is heavily accented in Italian. "But one day, when he wrapped his hands around her throat, as he always did when he was angry, the air choked out of his own lungs. He staggered away from her, and once more he could breathe. But every time after that, when he tried to lay his hands on her, he would choke."

"Like he was cursed," I muse, awe in my voice.

Father Patrick nods. "A year later, after a fit of rage because he could not hurt her, he turned his hands on me. Just a young boy, I thought I was dead. But finally he relented. The next morning, my mother woke up screaming."

He looks up at me, his eyes very calm, very even. "My father had choked to death in his sleep, and there were bruises around his neck in the shape of his own hands."

Goose bumps flash over my arms. I swear the temperature of the room has dropped ten degrees.

"When I went into the ministry, I spent my time looking for other cases like my father's. I sought out others who could not fully explain their experiences. I searched for acts of God that righted wrongs committed against the innocent."

"Have you found others?" I ask.

He nods and offers a small smile. "Oh, yes."

I blink.

I'm actually a little astonished. For centuries Cyrus has always promised he would find a way to break our curse, and while he has tried in the past, nothing has seemed solid.

But here, here is someone else who has had experience with them.

"And Grace has quite the story to tell as well," Cyrus says, nodding his head to her.

My eyes shift over to the older woman. She's black and her hair hangs long, in silver streaked dreadlocks. There are wrinkles that cut deep into the corners of her eyes.

"I worked as a nurse in Ganslaw, New Orleans for eleven years," she begins. Her accent is distinctly Southern, but it's different than Elle or Ian's. Deeper, with darker roots. "One night, every ambulance in the area was dispatched to an old, backwater church. The paramedics brought in eight men, and one dead little girl."

My stomach rolls. I don't even know much of the story, and already I feel sick.

"To this day, I do not know what those men did to that little girl," Grace continues, letting her eyes slide closed for a moment. "I did not want to know. But those men were brought in to the emergency room. Every one of them had blood pouring from their noses, their ears, and their eyes."

An image flashes across my vision, violent and gruesome, blood pouring from every opening.

"I was the managing nurse on duty that night," she continues her story. "And as I tried to help those sinners, as my hands were coated in their blood, I felt this...darkness creep inside of me. I could feel it attached to each and every one of them. It was as if we were connected. I don't know how to explain it. Almost like...the exact opposite of them being a brilliant light, a beacon in the dark. All I could see was their darkness."

I feel cold. So, so cold.

"I knew they were going to die that night. Like a ticking clock was inside of me. We never found what was wrong with those men," Grace says. "And one by one, throughout the night, each of them bled to death." She folds her hands on the table, staring off into the distance, not really seeing anything. "From then on, there would at times be individuals who came into the hospital, and I could feel that same darkness in them. Like the darkness that poisoned me that night would reach out and shake hands with the darkness in them. And I always knew within minutes when they were going to die."

"You can sense when a curse is going to claim someone?" I ask in a whisper. Emotion fills my eyes. I feel my entire body tremble.

We could know. We could have warning.

My eyes flick over to Cyrus. His expression is grave and his face is pale. I reach out and take his hand, clinging to it like it's my last lifeline.

We could have warning.

"I thought they could help us," Cyrus says. "They may not have the answers we need on how to break it, but it's a start."

A breath escapes my lips, a cry or a laugh, it isn't really quite either. "It's more than a start, Cyrus. It's more than we've had all this time."

There's timid hope in Cyrus' eyes. He reaches up, placing a hand on my cheek. I see his promises, and my heart swells at his action in keeping them.

He looks over at the two individuals. "We have many questions for you."

WE SPEND HOURS ASKING FATHER PATRICK AND GRACE questions. How many curses have they each encountered? Patrick's answer is twelve, and Grace says seven in addition to the men the night she made the connection with them. Of what nature have the curses been? Grace has never known very specifically, because they all died within hours of coming to her. Father Patrick's answers are varied. Anything between possession and the inability to consume food and the extreme fear of children.

Have either of them seen a curse broken?

They look at one another, as if afraid to give the answer. They each shake their head.

I lean forward, across the table. "Do you feel a timeframe when you look at me?" I ask Grace, begging her with my eyes to give me an answer.

Grace sits forward, studying me. Like she can read a date hidden somewhere on my skin, her eyes rove over me.

"I sense a recent death," she says, her brows furrowing. "Very recent. And not just that of a loved one. Your own."

I nod, but I can't offer anything else. Telling these two everything is just one more complication at the moment.

She accepts it, though. She continues studying me.

"When someone is close to death, I feel this...oppressive darkness. Like it's dropping down from the ceiling. It's heavy. It chokes the air out of the room. I've only ever detected death when it's been hours away." She sits back, looking from me, to Cyrus, and back to me again. "I don't feel that weight."

Cyrus actually lets out an audible breath. A sigh of relief.

I'm being a bitch when I think that's stupid. We've always had a bit of a warning before, when I starve and wither. I'm *obviously* not on the brink of death now.

"But I feel that darkness," Grace says. Her voice darkens, grows thicker. "Like I said, it's like a connection. Like there is a tether that stretches between me and it. I've never felt it so strong. The curse on the both of you…" She trails off, looking at us with darkness.

"I did something unforgiveable," Cyrus says. There's regret in his voice. It's quiet and ashamed. "A very long time ago. And I've spent years paying for my mistakes. As has my wife, even though none of it was her fault."

"I have seen it before," Father Patrick says. His words are at times difficult to understand, his accent is so thick. "That a victim has become a part of the curse. That they have had to pay for the sins of others."

"And have you ever found a way to help them?" Cyrus implores. His tone is desperate.

"We have lessened the symptoms," the man says, but there's something about the tone of his voice that makes me question if his words are true.

"Please," Cyrus begs. "Tell me what it is you did to do so."

Father Patrick sits forward, staring deeply into Cyrus' eyes. "You must seek forgiveness from God. Only then will he relieve your burdens."

Oh, no.

Oh, no *no no no no*.

As if in slow motion, I see Cyrus' expression change from that of grief and desperation, to rage. Unfiltered rage.

"Do you think that I have not tried that?" he bellows. He stands, slamming his fists down on the table. There's a great crack, and a huge split shoots down the table. "Do you think I have not spent decades of my life, praying to a being, asking for forgiveness for my sins? Do you think I have not served the penance of a thousand men seeking absolution?"

Father Patrick cowers back in his seat. He's bone white. His body trembles from head to toe.

As he should.

Cyrus' eyes have ignited brilliant red, and black veins sprout all over his face. The tendons in his neck strain out against his flesh. His fingers have dug holes into the table's surface.

"I brought you here because you made me believe you had answers for me," Cyrus seethes. "So tell me that you have other suggested methods beside begging God for forgiveness."

My stomach twists in knots. I feel so sorry for the man, and Grace, who looks scared, but not to the same level as Father Patrick. But the man...I'm sure he's bound to have a heart attack at any second.

But I feel the raging disappointment, too.

We need answers.

But this man has none.

"I..." he stutters. "I beg your forgiveness. This...this has been the only form of relief I have found in my years of research. Please…" he bows his head, fear trembling every inch of his body. "I beg your pardon, sir."

Cyrus' face is the physical depiction of rage. It isn't contained. He leaves it all on display.

"Get. Out."

Cyrus, too, trembles. He stares at Father Patrick with his eyes glowing brilliant and terrifying.

The man's eyes widen for just a moment, and I smell his fear peak once more. But he shoves back, knocking his chair right over.

He never takes his eyes off of Cyrus as he walks around to the end of the table, which points to the exit of the Great Hall. With one last look over his shoulder, Father Patrick turns, and runs.

I look back to Cyrus and see him staring down at the surface of the table. His breathing is hard and labored, and I know how hard he's trying to gain control once more. For ten full seconds, we all are frozen, waiting as Cyrus reclaims himself.

"You will live out the remainder of your life here at the castle," Cyrus says as his eyes flick up to Grace. "You will be generously compensated, and you will have a life of ease. But you are our only solid connection to a possible warning for my wife, and so I cannot allow you to ever leave. But I will make sure you are taken care of."

Cyrus turns and swiftly walks away from the table, aiming out of the Great Hall.

With my mouth hanging open slightly, I look from him and back to Grace.

She blinks twice, and I can tell, her brain is trying to

catch up to the life-changing words Cyrus just spoke. She opens her mouth, but no words come out.

My heart breaks for her, because in this, I know I won't be able to change Cyrus' mind.

Grace Stevens will live the rest of her life here at Court because Cyrus believes he can use her to gain a warning for when the end will come for me.

When it comes to me, he will do anything.

"I'm so sorry," I offer with the shake of my head. I stand, feeling a little lost. My brain is running a million miles an hour trying to sort out the ramifications of everything that's just happened.

"Don't..." I stumble over my words. "Don't try to leave." I look over at Grace. She looks surprised, taken off guard. But she doesn't look as terrified as I think she should. "I'll make sure you're taken care of. Just...don't try to leave, I beg you. For your own safety."

I take one step back, toward the exit.

"Take the stairs down the hallway," I say as I back away. "Go up to the next floor. Down the hall a little ways there are a series of bedrooms. You may take any of them you like as your own."

Grace stands, uncertainty and worry in her eyes.

"I'll be there to see you soon," I promise as I stop in the doorway. "I will figure this out. Please..." I beg once more, because I know what will happen if she doesn't listen to me. "Just don't try to leave."

If she does, Cyrus will make her pay.

He's in pain right now. He's disappointed.

Cyrus does bad things when he's experiencing those two

emotions.

Finally, I get the confirmation I'm so desperate for. Grace nods, and I see it in her eyes, she means it.

I listen, and a crash upstairs tells me Cyrus is in his office. Up the stairs I slip and down the hall. And then quietly, I step into the doorway.

There's a vase lying on the floor by the fireplace, shattered into a thousand irreparable pieces. It was old. Expensive. And now it's a ruin.

Cyrus stands in the middle of the room with his back turned to me. He breathes hard, his shoulders are tight. I can tell, he's ready to snap at any moment.

My initial reaction is to yell. To swear at him and demand *what the hell?* Logan wants to argue, Sevan wants to be angry at his extreme reactions and for hijacking that woman's life.

But I—as a whole person—someone who is many but one—I can't pretend that I don't know this man. I can't ignore thousands of years of knowing him, of being witness to his reactions. I can't pretend that wasn't the exact reaction I was expecting to what just happened.

I don't excuse Cyrus' behavior.

But I do understand it.

I step into the office and slowly cross the space. When I reach him, I tuck myself into his chest, wrapping my arms around his waist. I lay my head on his chest, listening to his heart race an angry sprint.

I tuck myself tighter to him as his arms come up and wrap around me. And I listen, count each beat, as his heart begins to slow.

Cyrus is a man of passion. He's so filled with it. He's a mountain filled with explosive gas, and all it takes is one small strike to make it all explode.

But here, in this small space of reality, he's just Cyrus.

He's just the man I love.

"There will be time to get more answers," I say without looking up. "I'm not going anywhere any time soon. We'll figure this out, together."

Cyrus tucks his face into my hair and squeezes me tighter. It's an admission of pain, of sorrow. Because for seven other lifetimes, we've spoken similar words. And we've never yet figured it out. We've never gotten answers.

"I just want us to be happy right now," I say as I look up at him. Cyrus' eyes are bloodshot, angry tear trails still wet on his cheeks. "I don't want us to feel desperate, because there is no need. I just want us to have normal, happy moments where we aren't worried about an end. It's just us here, Cyrus." I reach up, touching his face, cupping his cheek. "Just be with me, *im yndmisht srtov*."

Little by little, I see his eyes soften. And I know the power I have. Cyrus is capable of so much. He can change lives with just a few words. He's created something unimaginable. But with my own words, I calm the man. I sooth his tumultuous heart.

Together, here, I feel him calm. I feel our souls bend into one.

"I love you," Cyrus whispers, and his words are filled with pain and promises.

"I know," I answer.

CHAPTER 23

As I promised her I would, I help Grace Stevens get settled in. We have a long talk about what life here at Court will be like. I explain to her that those of us who live here are not like her, explaining as much as I can without fully disclosing what we really are.

She'll figure it out eventually. But that doesn't need to be right now.

We talk about her life back in New Orleans. To my surprise, she doesn't have any children, has never been married. Her life has been her work as a nurse.

That career is going to be difficult to give up.

But beside that, she doesn't seem all that concerned about the fact that she will never return to her life.

Then again, I think about that feeling she's described, about knowing when someone is cursed and how long it will be until they are claimed by it, and maybe this will be a relief for her. Maybe it's better that she only have to be exposed to the curse on Cyrus and I.

And then I'm back to dealing with the drama at hand.

Over the course of the next two days, I make phone calls to fifteen different Houses around the world. I explain to them that we have a few individuals here at Court that we aren't sure are trustworthy when it comes to our secret. I tell them that in the next day or two, they will be sent an individual who is to live in their House, and that they are to watch them for the rest of that Royal's life.

No, they will never have any Royal claim over the House they are sent to, and neither would any heirs they may ever produce.

No, they will never, ever be allowed back at Court, even to visit.

No, there is no choice in this matter.

So for the two days after that, the soldiers in the valley below us escort individual Royals to privately chartered jets, they point guns at them the entire flight to their destination, and then they are handed off to the Houses in their new parts of the world.

We shrink here at Court, but already, I feel the weight on my shoulders get just a little lighter.

Seventeen days after this "invasion" began, I know that the time has come.

It's time to release Alivia, Ian, and Eshan.

It's time to bring Mina, Fredrick, and Horatio back to duty.

As soon as it is dark, I slip down to the base and give word to Matthias and Dorian and Malachi. I ask that my grandsons escort the releases to the castle at midnight. Then I return to the castle.

I find Cyrus in the lab. I walk up behind him, wrapping my arms around his waist, hugging myself into his back.

He's reading some kind of ancient text. But I don't bother trying to decipher its words. That's not what I'm here for.

"I'm bringing some back to the castle tonight," I say. "Mina, Fredrick, Horatio. Eshan. And Alivia and Ian."

He lifts his head at that, his attention piqued at the names.

"I need you at my side," I say, cutting to the heart of my request. "You don't have to do anything. They don't even have to see you for more than a minute or two. But I do need them to see you. I need them to see with their own eyes that you're still alive and well. Because I need at least Alivia to take word back to the House of Conrath that she's seen you with her own eyes. So she can spread the word that you're still standing. Many of the Houses doubt me, and we can't have that show of uncertainty."

I turn my head, pressing my lips to the base of Cyrus' neck. His flesh is warm and soft. "I need you at my side when they come back tonight. Even if only for a minute."

Maybe he can hear my desperation. Maybe he can sense how tired I am.

But Cyrus turns, holding me against him. His eyes glow with intensity as he looks down at me.

"I will be there for you, my love," he says softly.

I smile in appreciation, rising onto my toes to kiss his lips.

TOGETHER, WE GET READY. I'M NOT REALLY SURE HOW TO dress. We need to show a strong front, for Alivia and her House's benefit and impression. But these are also people who are close to us, people who are going to be angry and hurt when I explain what I did to them.

I end up choosing a dark purple dress that hugs my bust and fans out from there, dropping to the floor. Not a chance I'm going to wear the crown today, but I do twist my hair up, regal and elegant.

Cyrus dresses in black slacks, a white button up shirt, and a vest.

Powerful, but not overbearing.

Still, my heart races in my chest as the hour ticks closer. With ten minutes to go, we go down the stairs.

Cyrus' hand reaches for mine, and my eyes whip over to him.

"It doesn't matter if they're angry, or if they understand," he says as we stop at the base of the stairs. "They may be important to you, you may even love them, but you have to think about more than just them. You did what you had to, my love."

Tears of gratitude well at the backs of my eyes, but thankfully do not shine in them. I nod once, bolstered.

It was exactly what I needed to hear.

Together, we cross the main floor and go to the front doors.

When the clock in the entry chimes midnight, I squeeze Cyrus' hand once more, and together, we each take one of the door handles, and pull them open wide.

KEARY TAYLOR

There, walking up the road, just twenty yards away, is a group of eight.

And the second their eyes land on Cyrus, every one of them stops dead in their tracks.

I take advantage of the stalled moment to observe every one of them.

Alivia and Ian seem no different than the day we were "invaded." Fredrick is as pale and thin as ever. Mina nearly looks bored, as if the past two weeks were merely an inconvenience. But Eshan... He looks thin. Pale. The bags under his eyes make me think he hasn't slept this entire time.

He only takes a moment, taking the both of us in. And then he breaks out into a sprint, dashing up the road.

He collides with me as he crashes into the castle. His thin arms wrap around my shoulders, hugging me tight to him. Startled, I hug him back, pulling him in close. Emotion pricks the backs of my eyes as I hold my little brother who is at least six inches taller than me.

Behind him, I hear footsteps again as the group once more finishes the journey to the castle doors.

"Your majesty," multiple voices murmur. Eshan releases me, and I see Mina, Fredrick, Dorian, Malachi, Horatio, Ian, and Alivia dipping in a bow.

There's awe in each of their faces when they look up at Cyrus.

Most all of them knew there should be a possibility that he would recover. But one wouldn't suspect that from the looks on their faces.

There's reverence there. Absolute awe.

"You're alive," Alivia breathes. And I see fear in her eyes.

Justified.

She saw the man staked, and then just moments later she was dragged here for a trial, accused of orchestrating it.

"It seems my curse continues to be stronger than anything," Cyrus says, fixing Alivia with dead eyes. "Even death."

I hate that fear and uncertainty in Alivia's eyes right now.

This needs to end.

"So is anyone going to explain why the two of you are here, in the castle, looking quite comfortable, while the rest of us have been wasting away down in the slums?"

Oh, Ian is too bold. Too stupid.

Does the idiot not know when it is the place and time for blunt words?

"Let's get inside," I say through gritted teeth. I nod my head further in the castle, my eyes flicking out to the complications outside. I close the castle doors and lead the group toward the Great Hall.

Eshan hovers at my side, and I reach my hand out, taking his in mine.

Guilt sparks in my throat when I look over at him.

He's sixteen. He's human. He's innocent in all of this.

It's my job to protect him. To guard him.

And look what I've just put him through. Because all I could think about in the last two weeks was Cyrus and our twisted hearts.

I go to the head of the table, Eshan on my one side, Cyrus standing at the other. I wait for everyone else to sit, but none of them do. They stand around the edges of it, and just look at Cyrus and I expectantly.

"I think the betrayals we've faced run deeper than anyone realizes," I begin. All eyes flick from Cyrus over to me. As he promised, Cyrus is at my side, and I can feel his support, but he doesn't say a word. "I think there are Born who have infiltrated Roter Himmel, but I also believe there are Royals here, maybe throughout the world as well, who want to see the monarchy fall."

I look around to each of the people that surround me. And I'm one hundred percent faking everything. My confidence. My bravado.

Really, inside, I'm flaking. Crumbling. I'm filled with doubt.

"We interviewed everyone here at Court and they swore their loyalty, but words are only words," I say. My throat grows tight as I close in on the words I don't want to admit to. "For the safety of the Court, for the safety of the world, I needed to find the truth."

"All of that down there was staged," Alivia concludes instantly.

I nod. "I needed to get down to the core of everyone here at Court. I needed them to have motivation to tell the truth when interrogated about our kind and their intent."

"So you used fear," Ian says, disgust seeping into his voice.

"Fear brings out the truth of people," Cyrus chimes in for the first time. And just his words, the hardness on his face, I see that fear instantly back in the eyes of all those that surround us.

"People lie, they can say anything they want, but that doesn't make it the truth," I move right along, feeling desperate. I don't like feeling like I have to explain myself, but it rises in me, choking me. "I didn't want to have to do this, to bring this on the people, but Cyrus was decapitated, there were people who came to my parents' house in Colorado and murdered them. The bloodshed would spread and if we did nothing, the entire world could fall apart in a matter of months."

"And you didn't trust us?" I'm surprised when it's Mina who speaks up. "After everything we've done, after the service we've devoted to not only Cyrus, but you, in the last few months?"

I have to remind myself, that she, and Fredrick, who looks just as betrayed and annoyed, they have never had to be under the rule of anyone but Cyrus. They don't know me. They don't trust me.

"You're all here, in the castle now, while everyone else is down there, because I do trust you," I say, keeping my voice level and calm. "I am sorry, really truly sorry I had to put you all through everything the last two weeks, but I needed the entire city to truly believe the invasion."

"We could have helped you, you know," Alivia says. She looks over at me with dark eyes. "What you had to deal with, what you had to coordinate, the stress you must have been under pulling everything together. We could have helped you."

I keep staring at her. The woman I look so much like. The woman who's been a leader for sixteen years now. The woman who finally brought the Queen back into the world.

I hate this disconnect I feel with her. I don't want it to be there.

But it is.

"I needed everyone to believe it was real," I reiterate. "I'm sorry for the stress I've put you all under. But I did what I had to do."

I reach out for Cyrus' hand. I take a step toward the door. "It might be hard, but I need everyone to go back to normal life. I need your help, your services. Alivia, I know you need to return to your House. As soon as our jets have returned from their errands, you can go home. In two days."

I look back at them one more time.

I'm fracturing. Because I see the looks of betrayal and hurt on every single one of their faces. They hate me right now. They hate seeing me holding Cyrus' hand for support. They hate him backing me up, and me not refuting anything he said.

Emotion pricks the backs of my eyes. But I have to hold it in.

I have to believe I made the right choices.

So I turn away. I hold my head high.

And side by side with Cyrus, we walk out of the room.

I only get twenty yards down the hall when I can't hold it anymore. The emotions well up inside of me like a tsunami. I let go of Cyrus hand. And I run.

Down hallways and passages. Cyrus doesn't yell after me, I know he won't, because that would alarm those back in the Great Hall, and he won't make me look weak right now. But he follows after me for a moment, and then he stops, realizing what I need.

I weave through the castle, the air rippling my hair behind me. I twist down one stairway, cut through a room, down a passage.

And finally I can't go any further.

I collapse in a room I don't even recognize. There's an overstuffed purple couch, a vanity, and a chandelier hanging above my head. I crumple into the couch, burying my face in my arms, and I let the sobs rip through me.

I'm only twenty-freaking-years old.

I'm not supposed to have to make these kinds of calls. I'm not supposed to have the power to control a kingdom and influence Houses around the world. I'm not supposed to have armies at my disposal.

I'm supposed to be out figuring my life out. I'm supposed to be worrying over how to pay rent. I'm supposed to be out for weekend parties with my best friend. I'm supposed to be worrying my mom when I don't check in often enough.

It's too much.

I feel like I'm drowning.

Because there are a dozen people somewhere in the castle who are livid with me. Who doubt me. Who think I did something dark and terrible.

I've done them.

I had to do those things.

But I'm tired. I feel guilty. I can't hold it all in anymore.

After holding it all on my own, I have to drop the strength. I have to drop Sevan.

So as Logan, alone in a dark castle, in a strange land, I sob. I mourn the life I've lost, and the fate in front of me that just feels too damn heavy.

CHAPTER 24

HOURS LATER, FEELING WEAK AND DEPLETED, I LEAVE MY sanctuary. Numbly, through the hallways, I walk, straightening my dress. I wipe the mascara lines running down my face. I fix my hair as best I can.

I rely solely on my sense of hearing and smell. Down the hall on the second floor I walk, listening for who is where.

I start with the hardest.

Eshan is lying in his bed with the TV on, digging into a bag of chips. The moment I walk inside, he sits up, clicking the TV off. He watches me with waiting, unsure eyes.

I cross the room, sitting on the edge of the bed.

"I came to apologize," I say, getting right to the point. "What I did was really terrible, and thinking of it now, I should have found a way to accomplish what I needed to without getting you involved."

He just stares at me, and it's hard to read his eyes at the moment.

"You're innocent in all of this, and your life has been thrown into chaos and it's totally unrecognizable now because of me." I look down into my lap and once more the guilt washes over me. "It's my job to protect you, and I failed, miserably, within the first week of being your guardian. So, I'm just really, really sorry."

Eshan doesn't say anything for a long minute, and when I finally look over at him, he just gives a shrug. "Whatever. At least I'm not stuck in that room anymore."

I raise an eyebrow at him. "Whatever? That's all you got for me?"

He shrugs again. "I mean, it was kind of a dick move and it was pretty intense and scary, but you didn't leave us down there forever. And look around, Logan. There are people plotting to kill you and Cyrus. I mean, you had to do something."

A little laugh slips past my lips. I shake my head at him, relief flooding through my shoulders.

"You're not supposed to make it this easy for me," I tease him.

"What?" he says. "You want me to give you endless crap?"

I laugh, shaking my head.

And then, twisting around, I launch myself at him, tackling him back to the bed and digging my fingers into his ribs, in his most ticklish spot.

"No!" he calls out in protest, writhing and twisting until he wiggles his way out from under me. He makes a dive, grabbing my ankle, tickling his own fingers against my bare skin. "You fight dirty, I will fight dirty back!"

I scream, yanking my foot out of his grip, which is only possible because I am not human any more.

And I know, even if no one else I go to apologize to forgives me, it's okay. Because my little brother's opinion is the only one that matters, and I can handle that.

An hour later, I head down the hall. The door at the end is where I hear the voices coming from. I knock on the door and wait.

Feet shuffle across the floor, and then the door swings open to reveal Ian.

He just glares darkly at me.

I push my way past him, going to stand in the big, beautiful room. And there's Alivia, packing things into a bag over by the ornately carved desk against the wall.

"I came here to apologize," I say, diving right in so as to avoid an argument with Ian. "I know it can't have been pleasant, being down there in the camp with all that stuff going on. I know you were probably scared and you didn't know what was going to happen. I'm sorry for that stress I put you both under."

"Stress?" Ian growls as he steps forward. "Stress is worrying if you've got money to pay your bills. Stress is worrying about if you forgot to turn the stove off. That-"

"Ian, go find something to do," Alivia cuts him off. She straightens, staring her husband down with annoyed and serious eyes. "I need a few minutes to talk to Logan. Alone."

He glares at her, and I remember what Elle and Christian told me. That this was just their way of sorting things out.

With a huff, he turns, and walks out the door.

We both stare at it for a good thirty seconds after he leaves, neither of us saying anything.

And then we turn to each other and start talking at the same time.

Then we both give a little laugh, at the same time.

"Look," Alivia says when I wait for her to speak. Her being my elder and whatnot... "You don't really need to apologize. Yeah, it sucked, and yeah, I kind of thought we were all going to die for a while and that my House would have no idea what happened to me. But..." She trails off, and I try to read what's in her eyes.

Surprisingly, it's understanding.

"Your plan was genius," she says as a little smile curls on her lips. "It was kind of insane, and I'm really not sure how you brought it all together in such a short amount of time. But it was brilliant."

I look at her warily. "Really?" I question. "You're not totally pissed at me and want to throw me off a cliff for keeping you all in the dark?"

Alivia sighs. She slides her hands into her back pockets, shifting her weight from one foot to the other. "I mean, yeah, I wish you had let me in on it so I could have helped you. But, I can't say that I wouldn't have handled it the same way."

We look at each other, and I finally realize—I've questioned if she's a good person or not the entire time I've known she is my birth mother—but am I a good person? Sometimes. But not all the time.

I have to concede, that's how we all are. We all have our moments in each direction.

"Stress makes you make extreme decisions, and some-times you get so caught up that it's hard to tell what's good and what's bad." Alivia studies me, and I wonder if she's seeing some of herself in me. "But there was a lot on the line, and in the end, sometimes all you can count on is yourself."

She crosses the space and takes my hands in hers. I look into her eyes, the biggest difference between us. "You've had multiple lifetimes to prepare for this. You can do this. You will make the right calls. And our world is lucky to have you." She takes a step back and dips into a bow. "Queen Sevan."

My heart breaks out into a sprint. It's so full of gratitude, and Alivia's words fill me with confidence and affirmation.

"Thank you," I say quietly as she straightens.

"Any time," she smiles. She turns, going back to the clothes she's packing. "Now, as much as I'd love to stay and help you with all of this mess, I really do think I need to get back to my House. These problems are bigger ones than I feel qualified to deal with."

I laugh at that, and then sigh for myself, because no one can deal with it but me. "I understand. The next jet will return in a day and a half. You and Ian can leave then."

Alivia nods, closing the bag, as packed as she can get it for now. "Now, can I ask? What's the deal with Cyrus?"

I tense up a little at that. My defenses rise, prepared to fight. "He's been through a lot. It shouldn't be surprising that he's easing back into things a little slowly. I'm happy to take the reigns for a while."

She shakes her head. "No, I didn't mean with that. I get it, Cyrus needs a break and all this drama isn't where his head is at. I meant with the two of you." She smiles. "I mean the epic love story of Cyrus and Logan."

She places a little emphasis on the word Logan, and I know what she's getting at.

Instantly I feel my face blush. I shake my head, dropping onto the bed behind me, and let myself flop back onto it, to stare at the ceiling.

"Is this what we're supposed to do, as mother and daughter?" I say, smiling as I stare up at the ceiling. "Talk about boys and our feelings?"

Alivia lies on the bed too, our bodies in a tee shape. "Well, we do have twenty years to make up for. And maybe we'll never be mother and daughter in the traditional sense. But I think we can be friends. At least I hope so. I mean, we do nearly look the same age."

I laugh at that and flop an arm over my eyes.

But really, it will be nice to talk to someone about it.

I've kind of lost Amelia. I don't have my own mom to talk to anymore.

"It's been a little challenging," I confess. "Cyrus came back the day of the solar eclipse."

I hear Alivia make this little sound, like *duh, of course.* But I move on.

"And it's been complicated, dealing with everything outside and holding it all together. But…" I consider my words. "But the last sixteen days have been some of the happiest of my life. Which doesn't happen for me."

Alivia reaches over, tucking her hand into mine.

"I know everyone has their ideas about him and experiences with Cyrus," I continue. "But it's so different when it's us. We do and don't take each other's crap. But mostly it's just...good. We're...we're really happy."

Alivia squeezes my hand. "I'm so glad to hear that." She takes a second to collect her thoughts before continuing. "Everything that happened between Cyrus and I ended up leading to pain, but I can say this: my heart has always ached for Cyrus. I don't think there's a person in the world that could have looked into his eyes and not seen his pain. I'm happy for him that he doesn't have to go through that anymore."

She means it. I can feel that.

So I squeeze her hand too, and for a few minutes, I can let all the weight on my shoulders go. I can just appreciate the moment of lying here, with a friend, talking about the man I've fallen in love with.

CHAPTER 25

As further apology, I plan a party. Partly, just to say sorry for seeming like a jerk who locked everyone up, and partly going away party for Ian and Alivia. It's a lot of work to plan on my own. Considering we still don't really have any staff around to help, it's just me and Eshan pulling it all together.

When I tell Cyrus my plan, he glowers at me, muttering something about having to be in the same room as Alivia.

"Okay," I growl. I turn in the closet, where I was digging around for something to wear tomorrow evening for the party. "This has got to stop. It's been how long since you and Alivia had your drama?"

"Sixteen years," Cyrus says, lifting his chin. I see his defenses bristling as I step up to the yelling plate.

"Exactly," I say, putting my hands on my hips. "We may not be the closest, and no, we'll never have a mother and daughter relationship, but I think I'm starting to like the woman, and she's always going to be a part of my life. So you and her need to get past this damn contention and get over yourselves."

I step forward, grabbing Cyrus' hand, and haul him toward the door.

"And just where do you think you're taking me, Logan?" Cyrus demands.

"We're having a sit down with the two of you, right now," I say.

I'm pushing Cyrus to his limit. I know I am. But I also know the influence I have over him, and if I have to, I'm going to use it over him if it means finally getting these two past this drama.

"What about this idea makes you think it's a good one?" Cyrus demands, though he doesn't pull his hand out of mine, and he doesn't try to stop me.

"It's my idea," I scoff. "Of course it's a good one."

I stalk down the hall toward Alivia's room and knock loudly. When she opens with a surprised expression, I grab her hand too, pulling her out of the room, and all three of us march down the hall.

"Lo..." Alivia stutters. "What...what is going on, Logan?"

"We're all going to have a little chat," I say, and that's all the explanation I offer as I march us down the hall, down the next floor, and straight into my office. I stuff the two inside, and close the doors behind the three of us.

I turn in place, glaring at the both of them.

"This little feud needs to end," I state. I fold my arms over my chest. "Today. Alivia might have toyed with your emotions, Cyrus, but I've also heard from a lot of sources that your reaction wasn't exactly level-headed."

Instantly, both of their eyes ignite red and their expressions contort with rage.

"She dared tell me she'd dreamt of castles," Cyrus seethes. "She dared to hold me close and whisper words that made me believe."

"Words, Cyrus!" Alivia snaps. She turns toward him, smacking her fist into the opposite palm. "Those were only words! You humiliated me, in front of Raheem, in front of Ian. In front of the whole Court!"

My initial instinct is to jump between the two of them, to force them to speak nicely and chill out.

But as they continue yelling, I realize that maybe this is what they actually need. After sixteen years of holding in this resentment, maybe they just need to let it all out.

"You used me to take care of that joke of a problem, Jasmine," Cyrus seethes in Alivia's face.

"You terrified me into taking my own life!" Alivia yells right back.

This entire fight is incredibly revealing. There are so many aspects of their time together, while Cyrus investigated if Alivia was Sevan or not, that I had no idea about.

"I warned Raheem, I warned you, that it would not be wise to pursue your attraction to one another," Cyrus hisses. "But the whore that you are, you let him risk his life and pulled him into dark corners and also whispered in his ear. And now I have forever lost my best spy."

"You took advantage of Raheem, and you know it," Alivia shouts back. "No, I shouldn't have led him on. But you didn't know that I was Sevan. You had no right to make the demands you did."

On. And on, they fight for over an hour.

I keep waiting for it, the moment when one of them will physically attack the other and I'll have to jump in and pull them off of each other. I'm sweeping the room with my eyes, looking for weapons they might use against each other.

Alivia won't be able to kill Cyrus, we've seen that proven multiple times now. But Cyrus could certainly put an end to Alivia.

But they just use words. The just keep screaming at each other.

I cringe a little. No wonder they hate each other so much. They did some really awful, terrible things to each other. Alivia certainly knows how to use words against someone. Cyrus certainly strikes back in physical ways.

He shattered Alivia's face once, apparently, when she accused him of not knowing what love was, saying he didn't know what love was considering what he did to me.

Ouch.

It rolls on for another half an hour, and even I'm getting exhausted.

Finally, there's a lull in the accusations. So I step forward, standing just three feet from the two of them.

"Now that you've gotten all of that out of your systems, I want to ask you something." I look from Alivia, to Cyrus. "All of that shit that happened between the two of you, what does *any* of it matter now?"

Alivia and Cyrus quickly look at one another, each of

their eyes widening for a moment, and then narrowing in thought.

"Cyrus, does it matter that she said those things to you, that she led you to believe she might be someone she wasn't, now that I'm back?" I ask.

He can't seem to find words. He stares at Alivia. His lips are slightly parted, but nothing comes past them.

"Alivia, I think you understand Cyrus' pain, and while what he did to you was terrible, do you not understand it to some degree?"

This side is harder to argue.

"Cyrus, does Alivia ever need to be afraid of you, now that I'm back?" I say the words firmly.

His eyes shift over to mine. And as he looks at me, I see his gaze soften. I see a deeper regret forming in them. I see the present and commitment there in them.

"No," he says quietly as he stares at me. His brows furrow, and I think he finally realizes now. His gaze shifts back to Alivia. "She's right. It was painful then. But..." He shakes his head and looks back to me. He reaches out, and I gladly take his hand. "None of it matters now."

Alivia continues to glare at Cyrus. The hurt in her direction won't be so easily forgotten. Not when he held her prisoner here for over a month, left to rot. Not when he branded her and her House. Not when he twisted not only her heart, but Raheem's, and Ian's as well.

"I think I've been waiting for more backlash for sixteen years," Alivia admits. "I've been waiting for you to show up at my doorstep and torture everyone in my House again because the memory of what happened between us might surface. I've been living in a degree of fear for a long time, Cyrus."

His gaze floats back to Alivia, and I see, he's now realizing the power and influence he's always held. He's been thousands of miles away from Alivia, on the other side of the world, but she's lived in constant fear of him.

He's held an ache in his heart over what she did. But it's nothing in comparison to the panic and fear she's dealt with for so long.

"Our feud is over, Alivia Conrath," Cyrus says. The words aren't easy for him to promise, I can hear it in his tone. "Unless you give us further reason to doubt your commitment to our kind, you have no more to fear from me."

I see it in her eyes. Like something lifts out of them. Like the burden of her fear just rose off her shoulders and dissipated into the air.

"I'm sorry I made you hope," she whispers as emotion rises in her eyes.

"I'm sorry I was such a tyrant."

Those may be the biggest words I've ever heard Cyrus speak.

And it's a huge miracle I'm witness to, when Cyrus reaches his hand forward, and Alivia shakes it.

Holy shit.

I think I was just witness to the ending of an era.

CHAPTER 26

I SLIP THE RUBY RED DRESS OVER MY HEAD AND STRAIGHTEN it around my body. It hugs me everywhere, in all the right ways. Even I smile a little as I look at myself in the bathroom mirror, taking in the back of the dress, which is ruched and highlights my features nicely.

"May I help you with that?"

Cyrus' voice purrs from the bedroom. He steps into the bathroom, heat and hunger in his eyes.

I blush and smile, turning my back to him.

He takes hold of the zipper, very, very slowly sliding it up. He leans forward, pressing a kiss to my bare shoulder. Electricity sparks in my blood, in my brain, in my lower belly.

As he tops the zipper off, I turn, bringing my hands up behind his head. I lace my fingers together, trapping him in my embrace.

"The way you look tonight, Logan," Cyrus growls, touching his forehead to mine. "I don't think I can let you out of this room."

I smile, tilting my lips up to his. I don't kiss him, I simply let my lips brush against his, teasing the both of us. "You don't look too bad yourself."

It's true. He wears a suit. Black trousers tailored to fit him precisely, a stark white shirt with a black tie. Black vest, and black suit jacket that highlights every dip and bend of his body.

I want to devour him.

I reach up, caressing his face. And as if Cyrus can't wait any longer, he dips his mouth to my neck, nipping and sucking, claiming me as his, forever and ever.

"There's a party downstairs that I'm supposed to be hosting," I say through a blissful smile.

"They can entertain themselves," Cyrus growls. "Fredrick is a very talented singer. Let him take over the evening's plans."

"Oh?" I groan as he kisses his way across my throat to the other side of my neck. His fingers tighten in my dress, pulling me closer. "I had no idea."

He makes an affirmative noise, but doesn't stop claiming my skin.

I give a lustful little moan but then push him back, taking his hand in mine. I use my best bedroom eyes when I look back at him, teasing him over what is to come later.

I don't really know what is to come later. I still haven't mentally been able to make myself move on from kisses and wandering hands.

"It's rude to be fashionably late," I tease when he tries to pull me back and keep me in the room. "And I *will* make you pay if you mess up my hair."

This makes him smile. He pulls me back in for one more quick kiss, and then follows me out of the bedroom and into the hall.

Music floats to our ears when we reach the stairs. The scent of food makes my stomach growl when it wafts its way through the stone hallways. I hear voices chatting off in the distance.

"I want to thank you," Cyrus says as we walk hand in hand toward the party. "For what you did, with Alivia and I. It was a conversation neither of us ever would have had on our own, but I feel…a sense of relief, now that we have."

"You're welcome," I say with a smile. He kisses me once more before we round the hall.

I could stay here with him all night, his hands wandering, mine clinging to every muscle of his frame. But this is a going-away party, and I must say my goodbyes—and apologies.

So, hand in hand once more, we turn, and walk through the huge, double doors into the parlor.

The room is dripping with gold and all the soft surfaces are velvet red. A golden chandelier with tinted crystals hangs from the high ceiling. Mirrors are hung all along the walls, making the room feel bigger and more crowded than it actually is. The side tables at the ends of each couch or chair are gold-plated.

The furniture is elegant and expensive. Crushed red

velvet makes them seem soft and inviting. A lavish rug is spread over the black marble floor.

The room is decadent. Over the top.

But it fits the mood of the night.

It took us a while, but after inquiring with first Dorian and Malachi, and then Matthias, Eshan and I found three soldiers who were said to be fabulous cooks. Looking at the spread on the table at the back of the room, I know we weren't misled. They're nowhere to be seen now.

Eyes turn to Cyrus and I as we enter, and I find that everyone has already arrived.

Alivia looks stunning in a solid black dress that accents her thin figure. Ian sports a tuxedo. Eshan and Fredrick look pretty dashing in their own suits, as does Horatio. And Mina wears a black leather number that fits her to a T. Dorian and Malachi are dressed in the fashion of the area they reside in.

It's a relaxed night. I make a speech, thanking them each individually for the ways they have helped me over the last few weeks or months. I raise my glass of blood to each of them in a toast.

It feels like it's too easy, to gain their forgiveness. Because each of them smiles, raising their glasses to me, as well. We all sit together, as friends, and enjoy the delicious meal prepared by hands that have pretended to hold us all captive.

The conversation is light and easy. There are smiles and jokes.

Until Eshan speaks up with his ignorant words.

"So, we all saw it," he says, looking down the table at

Cyrus. "Your head was cut clean off. Were you dead all that time, or just taking the world's best nap?"

There's seven different intakes of breath. Everyone sits back in their seats just a bit. And all eyes snap down to Cyrus, because every one of us is dying to know.

I've been meaning to ask the question, but I just haven't been able to make myself form the words.

Eshan immediately realizes his mistake, that he took things too far and too casually. His face immediately pales and he shrinks back in his seat.

But the words are out, and Cyrus can't ignore them.

I look at the man seated beside me.

His eyes take on a dark tone, and he looks up around at everyone from beneath his eyelashes. He twirls his fork in his hand, and then gently lays it down on his plate.

"I've never experienced death, even after all these years," he says finally. "So I cannot say that I know what it feels or looks like. But I do not believe that was where I was."

There's a silent beat. And collectively I can nearly hear us ask, *then where were you?*

"While Sevan worked to bring me back," Cyrus continues, reaching over to take my hand, "I felt as if I were here. I wandered Roter Himmel. I searched for a way back. I visited all the familiar places. I felt like I was lost. Except when she found me."

Cyrus' eyes rise up to meet mine, and my heart trips over itself.

"You remember me there with you?" I breathe.

The dreams. The strange, strange dreams where I always found him.

They were real. Somehow I'd traveled to him, found him in the limbo he was trapped in.

"Oh, yes," he confirms. The sincerity in his eyes tells me the truth of the words he speaks. "I would have stayed lost in the smoke forever if you hadn't come for me, Logan."

Emotion pricks at my eyes and I reach forward, touching his face. I bite my lower lip in an attempt to keep all of the emotions inside of me.

"Nothing could have dragged me back into this world of chaos and struggle, besides you, *im yndmisht srtov*." The way Cyrus looks at me, I feel as if he's scooped me into his hands and cradles me, safe and tender. Like my entire world only consists of Cyrus and me.

He raises my hand and presses a kiss to the back of my knuckles.

"And the legend of Cyrus and Sevan deepens," Alivia says, reminding me that we're surrounded by people.

I blink, looking around. Everyone is staring at us. So I smile, and let the evening move on.

But as I turn back to my meal, I continue to hold Cyrus' hand beneath the table, unable to let go.

It's agony, having to be normal and interact with every-one. Because every part of my brain is occupied by Cyrus, as he leans over, pressing a kiss to my shoulder. As my hand rests on his thigh, creeping more inward and higher. He leans in and whispers in my ear, and I let my lips brush his own as I quietly tell him that I love him.

I'm overwhelmed with love and want.

The evening rolls on, we finish our meal, and my heart breaks out into a flutter of excitement and anticipation when

Cyrus takes me by the hand, tugging me toward the doors that open up to a huge balcony.

Where the moon was full just weeks ago with the solar eclipse, it is now a thin sliver. But the stars are out, shining incredibly bright, twinkling.

A soft breeze pulls at my hair, and flutters the scent of pine and lemongrass our direction. Out in the distance, I can still see all those tents where I know our people are under the control of the army. But I look past them. I see the lake, glittering the reflection of the stars. I see the mountains. I see the trees. I see lazy clouds floating through the sky.

I lean against the railing, a contented sigh slipping past my lips.

Cyrus stands behind me, running his hands down my arms, slipping all the way down my skin until his fingers lace into mine. He presses a gentle kiss to my shoulder and I smile, leaning back into his warmth.

Cyrus tilts his head down, brushing his lips against my ear. "I have fallen completely and irreversibly in love with you, Logan," he says in a whisper. "From the first day I saw you, I wanted you. And every day since, I crave your presence. I love your strength and determination. I admire your commitment and your tenderness."

I lean into him, my cheek to his, relishing in the skin-to-skin contact.

"I love you with every part of my heart, Logan," Cyrus says intimately. His voice drops lower until it is a whisper.

"Will you marry me?"

My heart skips and my eyes fly open. I instantly twist, to get a better look at his face, to read his expression.

But as I turn, he reaches into his pocket, and at the same time, drops down onto one knee.

Holding my eyes with every ounce of seriousness in the world, he stares up at me. He holds out a ring.

Emotions prick the backs of my eyes and my stomach does this complicated quiver. My hands come to my chest, trying to calm the frantic storm inside of me.

"I told you once, even though the words were the hardest I've ever had to speak," he says. "I have never, ever fallen for another. My heart has always been Sevan's. But you came into my life Logan, and for the first time, I fell for another." His eyes are bright. I see the truth in them. "I love you, Logan Pierce. Do you think you could ever tolerate spending the rest of forever with a man as broken and imperfect as me?"

I bite my lower lip as moisture pools in my eyes.

"Logan," Cyrus breathes. "Will you marry me?"

And I can't hold it in any longer. The smile that splits my face could blind every Born or Royal in the world. "Yes," I breathe as a single tear breaks free. "Yes, yes, yes."

I rush him as he stands, wrapping my arms around his neck, clinging tightly to him. I feel his smile physically warming me. I feel like I'm glowing. Like I could float right off of this balcony.

Cyrus takes half a step back, taking my left hand in his. And he slides the most beautiful ring I've ever seen onto my finger.

A deep green emerald sits in the middle, oval shaped, and the exact same shade as Cyrus' eyes. A gold band encircles it, two infinity shapes on either side of the main stone. Small, white diamonds are laid into the band.

It catches the starlight beautifully.

"It's incredible, Cyrus," I breathe, admiring it. I can hardly catch my breath.

He brings his fingers to my chin, tilting my face up to his. And he kisses me. Slow. Gentle. It's a kiss that reaches from my lips, all the way down to the furthest corner of my soul.

It's a kiss I'll remember for the rest of my life.

The first kiss I share with my fiancé.

Not husband. Because that was when he was Sevan's.

Now he is mine.

Together forever: Logan and Cyrus.

I back away, looking into those eyes of his that match the jewel on my ring. "I love you, Cyrus. I swear I'm going to love you always, even when you're being a presumptuous pain in the ass." We both laugh and he looks at me tenderly from beneath his eyelashes. "Even when you're saving me from myself. I promise I will always love you."

He kisses me again. I could stay here forever, connected with the man who I thought had wrecked my life when he came into it, but really, he was just breaking his way into my bitter heart.

Gently, Cyrus takes my hand, backing me toward the doors again.

When we step inside, every single person is facing us. Smiles are plastered on their faces, and they raise a glass in our direction.

I feel my face blush red hot, but a smile breaks over my

lips. I raise my newly-ringed hand up in front of my face. "I said yes!" I squeal like a fifteen-year-old girl.

Everyone breaks out into cheers and clapping and congratulations.

Cyrus looks the happiest I've ever seen him as I look up at him and he smiles down at me. He pulls me in tight, his hands possessive, and kisses all sense out of me.

CHAPTER 27

AT THREE IN THE MORNING, GOODBYES ARE SAID, AND I GO
to change, and then I take one of the cars from the garage
underneath the castle, and I head toward the airport with
Alivia and Ian.

"I feel like I should be staying to help you deal with
everything going on," Alivia says when we're only ten
minutes from the airport. "I know how stressful dealing with
everything can be, and I had a House to help me."

I shake my head. "I'll be fine. I have Dorian and Malachi.
And Mina and Fredrick. And Cyrus."

Which isn't exactly true, but still.

"You need to get back to your own life," I say. "I appreciate you coming to help me identify Lorenzo."

"I still think you should be careful with him," she says,
looking out into the dark night. "Something about him and
what he says happened doesn't sit right with me."

I nod in agreement. "I will."

I turn off the main road and cut down the narrow drive that leads to the small airport. We drive past hangars, most of which belong to Cyrus or the members at Court. We roll past them, and I aim the car for the jet waiting on the tarmac.

The pilot and staff are waiting for them, standing straight and ready just to the side of the stairs.

"Enjoy your peaceful time back in Mississippi," I say with a smile, standing awkwardly in front of them while the attendants load their luggage.

Alivia laughs. She shakes her head, stepping forward. She wraps her arms around me in a tight embrace. "I know this might take some time to resolve. But I hope we get some more time together in the near future. I really want to get to know you better, Logan. Under circumstances that aren't so dire."

I do tense up. The thought makes me nervous. But still, I do nod. "I'd like that. Someday."

She backs up just a bit, and places her hands on either side of my face, staring into my golden green eyes. "There's no one in the world who can handle all of this like you can. I believe in you, Logan."

My throat tightens a bit at her words. But I give her an appreciative smile.

She releases me, and Ian steps up. He offers an awkward smile, and to my surprise, he actually hugs me.

"I might still be just a little bitter, about a lot of things," he says. "But I guess I just forget what responsibility and stress does to a person. You're not so bad, Logan."

I huff a laugh. "Thanks, I guess. You're not too terrible, either."

He releases me, and I offer a little wave as they both walk up the stairs to enter the jet.

Alivia looks over her shoulder one last time, and I smile at the woman who looks just like me. The woman who carried me for nine months. The woman whose name I didn't even know for twenty years.

But a woman who's been through a lot, and came out as an incredibly kind person. Someone who is a good leader.

Someone I now respect.

The pilot follows them inside, and then the door closes.

I don't know when I'll ever see Alivia again. But even if I never get to see her again, I'm happy with the time we got. It wasn't sweet and tender. But it was real and raw.

I feel the air warming as the sun rounds the globe, heading our way, but still an hour and a half off. Standing on the tarmac, I wrap my arms around myself and watch the jet taxi out onto the runway.

Through the dark, I hear the engines roar. The jet slowly inches forward, and gains speed with each second. And then it lifts off, bound on a journey halfway around the world.

It's weird, but I feel a small sense of relief as I climb into the car, alone, like having Alivia and Ian here was this weight in the back of my brain, constantly putting pressure on me.

Now I can just focus on the problems at hand.

Alone, I point the car back in the direction of Roter Himmel.

Traffic heading through this canyon is nonexistent. There is nothing through it besides Roter Himmel. So when I see taillights up ahead, two sets of them, my brows furrow. For ten minutes, I follow them through the dark and winding canyon, wondering if maybe they have a cabin off a side road up here somewhere.

But they never turn off anywhere. Straight and sure they drive toward my home, sending my heartbeat racing.

When we're only one mile from the crest of the canyon, where the view opens up to the valley, I know I can't wait any longer.

They'll see Roter Himmel in just minutes.

I lay my foot on the gas, switching to the opposite lane. I rocket down the road, driving side by side with the first car, and then surpassing it. And then I pull up alongside the front car.

Pressing a little harder on the gas, risking the sharp turns and curves of the road, I shoot ahead of the front car.

Recklessly, I angle my car across both lanes and instantly slow the car. I watch over my shoulder, making sure the cars behind me slow.

They do, but the nose of the front car only misses me by inches when I slam to a stop.

Looking down the road again, I barely see a break in the trees. Out across the way, I see mountains, and just barely in the dark, I see a spire—the castle, and one single light glowing dimly.

I get out of the car, slamming the door closed behind me.

But not before I slipped two stakes up my pant legs.

The window rolls down on the driver's side of the front car. And I slow as I walk up to her. Because even in this dark, nearly nonexistent light, I can see her eyes.

Golden jade, just like mine.

"Is something wrong?" she asks with a thick Italian accent. "Do I have a taillight out?"

Don't let her eyes distract you, I internally hiss at myself.

I straighten my shoulders, stopping beside her car. "I wanted to ask where you're headed."

I take a deep breath as I lean down, looking into the car. There are four others inside with her. They're all vampires. I can smell it.

"We're in the area, going to visit family," she says with a wary smile.

"And where does this family live?" I continue interrogating the woman.

"Do you treat all Royals who come to visit Roter Himmel with this much wariness?"

Holy shit. There it is.

No more beating around the bush.

"If you were Royals, I would think you would have heard the news by now," I say. I place my hands on the ledge of her window, staring her down with no fear. "Roter Himmel is on lockdown. No visitors in, no residents out."

I see something flash across her face, but it's difficult to identify. Relief. Fear. Surprise. "Well, that explains why we haven't been able to reach him." There's grit in her voice. It's angry, frustrated. But I can tell she's trying hard to control it. "We've traveled a long way to see our father. He asked us to come visit him. It was not easy to coordinate a visit involving this many family members."

Something twists in my stomach. A little warning bell sounds in the back of my brain.

I know the answer to the question I'm about to ask.

"And who is your father?"

She stares back at me with the same eyes as my own. "Lorenzo St. Claire."

Looking in the car again, I see the same yellow-green eyes staring back at me from the other four people in the car. And something tells me that the others in the car behind this one will be the same.

Shit.

Shit.

I don't know what this means.

I force myself to wear a poker face. It has to be a good one. But no matter what, I can't hide my eyes.

"I'm afraid that the lockdown hasn't been lifted," I say. "So I cannot allow you into the city yet. But there is a nice little inn about twenty miles back. You can stay there until all of this is over, on my bill."

The woman's eyes narrow, and there's just the faintest hint of red that ignites in them. But she keeps it under control. Good, for her safety. "And under what authority do you command us to stay outside of the city of our father?"

My eyes narrow. "That of the crown."

There's a faint little smirk that ignites in her eyes at that. "From what I hear, the King is dead. It seems to me the crown no longer has any authority if he is dead."

My hand darts forward and I feel my eyes light brilliant red. "It is under the authority of the crown of Queen Sevan, my crown, backed by King Cyrus, who is alive and well and will end any who dare trespass while we sort out Court business."

She stares at me with wide eyes and the others in the car hiss. One of the back doors opens and a man gets out.

I shove the woman back against her seat. I stalk around the car, coming nose to nose with the man. "As Royals, I know that you know what happens when you go against the crown." He backs up one step as I stand as tall as I can, channeling every ounce of rage and authority in me into my burning eyes. "The King and I will be happy to speak to you all, but not until the time is right. Not on Roter Himmel soil. So you either turn these cars around, go back to the inn, or I will have an army chasing you down in exactly one minute, and they will tear you limb from limb and will crucify your remaining trunk on the trees that guard the city. Do you understand?"

The man backs up one more step, and I do actually see fear creeping into his eyes.

With a wary look, he nods.

I turn to the others, glaring darkly at them all. "Go to the inn. I will be there soon to speak to you. But I warn you, if any of you steps one foot inside the borders of Roter Himmel, you won't survive, and the process *won't* be quick."

The woman in the driver's seat glares at me with hatred, but also fear. I stare her down, wishing I could crush her, until she gives me what I want. A nod.

The man gets back in the car. It's apparent the people in the car at the rear could hear us, because it backs up and flips around. And then they both head back down the road.

I stand on the road, watching their taillights head back in the direction we came from.

A terrified sigh quivers its way out of my lungs.

This is bad. This means something.

I don't believe for one second that Lorenzo just asked his other undisclosed Royal children out in the world to come visit him, and so conveniently soon after word of Cyrus' "death" began to spread around the globe.

I don't trust an inch of it.

I fish my phone out of my pocket and hit a name, holding it to my ear.

"Malachi," I bark the second he answers. "There's been some developments. I need twenty Court members you're certain we can trust. I know we haven't finished vetting like I want to, but there isn't time right now. I need twenty bodies at the mouth of the canyon. Now."

With an affirmative noise from him, I hang up.

I pace the road, looking every direction, straining my ears. Listening for any signs that the group of Lorenzo's descendants tries to sneak through the woods and into the city borders.

Six minutes later, I hear darting feet down the road in the city, and then just seconds later, a herd of blurs stops at my side.

"I do not have time to explain everything that has been going on," I say, standing before the twenty men and women my grandsons deemed trustworthy. "You'll be given all the answers in time, but for now, your Queen needs your help."

I explain what just happened, in small detail. I do name names, that of Lorenzo, and telling them they can identify his children by their eyes, the same of the man each of them already knows.

"I don't want a single one of them setting foot in our

city," I say. "Not until we have answers as to why they're here, and why now. Is that understood?"

"Yes, your majesty," they each say, offering a humble bow.

"I'll be back to the inn in a few hours," I say. "Keep watch over them for now. Stay in the dark. I want to know what they're up to. What they talk about."

I turn, angling toward the car once more. But I turn back. "I cannot thank you enough, for your loyalty to this family. To our kind."

I bow to them. Eyes grow wide and surprised in the dark.

Trusting them is all I can do. So I get in the car, and I race down the road, back into Roter Himmel.

CHAPTER 28

I PACE BACK AND FORTH OVER THE WOOD FLOORS OF MY office. Expectantly, Dorian, Malachi, Mina, and gratefully—Cyrus, watch me.

I need time to think. I need some time to figure all of this out and decide what the hidden agenda here is. But there is no time. They're here, just outside our borders.

"Right now Lorenzo has no idea about anything," I think out loud. "He doesn't know Cyrus is still alive. He doesn't know the invasion is fake. He doesn't know his children are here."

I stop, placing my hands on the desk. My brain is racing a million miles an hour and it's making me feel physically tired already.

"I think we need to make it known to these descendants that we have an army here. We need them to see it. They won't dare try anything if they see the manpower we have right now."

I stand, staring at a painting of Cyrus and I from the sixth century, but not really seeing anything.

"It needs to be me who shows them," I conclude. "We need to seem strong. I need them to know that they have to respect me and the crown."

I head toward the door, nearly forgetting there are others here. I stop suddenly, turning back. "Dorian, I want you to watch Lorenzo. Let rumors start spreading that a bunch of Royals with eyes like his have shown up and are trying to get into the city. I want to see what he does. And his four children who live here."

"Yes, my Queen," he acknowledges with a bow.

"Malachi, I want you and Mina to finish vetting the rest of the Royals. It's time to throw some real fire underneath this investigation. Wrap it up, because we're going to need those we can trust. I can feel it."

Malachi and Mina nod, standing, prepared to go and do what I've asked.

My eyes flick to Cyrus.

I need him.

I need the support right now. I need someone to talk this through with.

But I know he needs time out. I promised that I would carry this for now.

So I don't say anything to him. I turn, and head down the hall, heading straight for our room.

I can't tell if this is anxiety or relief I feel when I hear footsteps following behind me, recognizing the sounds of Cyrus. But I don't turn, don't say a word. I walk with focus up to the first floor.

Yanking the doors open, I go straight for the closet. I peel clothing off, digging through the closet. I pull on a pair of leather pants and a stake-proof vest, slipping a black shirt over the top of it.

Cyrus watches me, standing at the foot of the bed.

There's something going on in that head of his. I can feel the wheels turning, spinning.

But I don't have time to stop and ask what he's thinking.

Going to the bathroom, I tie my hair back, twisting it into a bun that will be out of the way if everything about to happen comes to a fight.

Crossing back into the bedroom, I go to the painting, swinging it aside. I press the third stone down. Then I twist the lantern hanging from the wall forty-five degrees to the left.

I flip aside the rug and pull the hatch open to the armory beneath our room. I drop down inside.

Above, I hear Cyrus get up and cross to the closet. I can hear him rummaging around. But I have to focus. I can't be Cyrus' fiancé right now.

I have to be the Queen of all vampires.

Sweeping the personal armory, I grab two aluminum stakes, lightweight but strong. I slip them into the waistband of my pants. I also grab a handgun, check to make sure it's loaded. And then for good measure I take five vials filled with purple liquid. I have no idea what they do, but if they're here, they have to be deadly. I slip them into the side pocket of my pants.

I turn to climb back out, when Cyrus suddenly drops down into the space with me. Without looking at me, he too loads up on weapons. He's dressed in similar clothing, but with no stake-proof vest, because as we've been witness to, he doesn't need it.

"Cyrus," I question. "What-"

Finished packing his weapons, he turns to me, his eyes intense. "When I woke up, all I cared about was our time together, Logan," he says. There's so much passion in his tone, I find myself leaning in closer. He takes my hands, holding them to his chest. "All I cared about was you. But I have seen what the weight of carrying all of this on your own is doing to you, *im yndmisht srtov*. And I've come to learn this, after all these years, because *you* have shown it time and time again: when you love someone, you carry one another's burdens."

My heart flutters and breaks into an elated sprint.

Cyrus reaches up, cupping his hand to the back of my head, touching his forehead to mine. "I am with you, my love. We will get our family through this. Together."

I rush forward, crushing my lips to his, gratitude and relief flooding through me.

I can do this. I know I can carry the kingdom through this trial.

But doing it alone is exhausting.

If we're going to be man and wife, we must be partners. Equals in carrying the burden of the crown.

"Thank you," I whisper against his lips as Cyrus clings to me, holding me with strength and possession.

He pulls away, looking deep into my eyes. "Let's go put this problem to bed."

I feel as if I could control fire and tempests as, side by

side, Cyrus and I walk out of the castle. I feel strong enough to crush the mountains that surround us as we dart invisibly fast over the valley. Together, I feel like we could command the moon to move and the sun to rise as we charge up the road, toward the mouth of the canyon.

A flash of irritation pulses through me as the sun crests the mountain and I have to pull on my sunshades. After two thousand years, the freaking sun itself is still one of our biggest downfalls.

As Cyrus and I approach the inn, we slow, searching the surroundings and listening for our spies.

Through the woods, I spot one of our men. Silently, Cyrus and I creep to him. And I forget, they all still think Cyrus is dead. So the man's eyes widen as he takes in Cyrus, his face blanching stone white.

"Report," I whisper. There's no time for shock or explanations.

"They haven't said much of anything," the man says. "Only expressed annoyance that they aren't being allowed into the city. The only thing said that raises any flags is that they've talked about the arrival of the rest of the family."

"The *rest* of the family?" I question, looking at Cyrus. "How many kids could Lorenzo possibly have? There were four in Roter Himmel, there's me, and now these ten? Who, besides our son has ever had so many children?"

Fifteen children, and apparently there are more?

"The House of Himura has many children," Cyrus says, thinking on it. "Dorian and Malachi, obviously, but that's been over all this time. Lorenzo has been around for only a fraction of that same time."

A fraction. Ha. That sounds absolutely ludicrous to Logan. Lorenzo has been around for over six hundred years according to Cyrus.

"Any idea how many more family members we're talking about?" I ask the spy.

He shakes his head.

"How has this slipped by?" I ask, turning back to Cyrus. "It's always been the same. The Royals here at Court function as members of our society. All Royals out in the world are in charge of a House, but I know there isn't a St. Claire House. But with so many of them..."

"They have the numbers to form one, easily," Cyrus growls. Embers glow in his eyes. As if it is a physical thing, I can feel the heat and anger growing from him.

"Keep watch," I instruct the spy. "Watch the roads, keep an eye on the mountains. If there are more coming, I want to know."

The spy nods and heads back into the trees.

"Shit," I breathe, turning back toward the inn and stalking toward it.

This is bad. This is big. And I don't understand enough of it.

I shove my way through the front door of the inn, and to my relief, I find the woman from the car at the front desk, trying to communicate with the desk clerk, who does appear to speak English or Italian.

"We need to have a talk," I say, fixing our mystery woman with my dark eyes.

Her own dart from me, to Cyrus, and they widen with absolute fear.

"Do you have a meeting room here?" Cyrus asks the desk clerk in perfect German.

The poor thing. She's just too helpful and innocent. She takes us down the hall and opens a door, revealing a small conference room.

"Thank you so much," Cyrus says, holding the door for the St. Claire woman and I. "We will make sure that every-thing is taken care of here. You should go home, and tell the rest of the staff to take the next few days off, as well."

He reaches into his pocket and pulls out a thick wad of cash, handing it to her. She gapes at him with wide eyes, the money sitting in her hand. Cyrus stares at her darkly, a million unspoken words of warning in them.

She swallows once, and then nods. She instantly goes back to the desk, grabs her purse, and walks straight out.

Cyrus shuts the door with finality, sealing us in.

I sit across from the woman. She's stark white. She keeps staring at Cyrus, and I can just see the gears turning in her head a million miles an hour.

"Tell me your name," I ask first. I lean forward, never breaking eye contact, even though she keeps looking at Cyrus, like he is the devil himself walked into the room.

"Irene," she provides. She swallows once and sits back in her chair. I hear her take two deep, slow breaths, like she's trying to get a grip on herself.

"We have a few questions for you, Irene St. Claire," I say. I lay my hands on the table, one on top of the other. "And you're going to answer them honestly, got it?"

She just stares at me, her lips frozen.

Cyrus pulls out the seat beside me and sinks down into it.

I swear, I can feel heat radiating off of him. Fear ripples off of him on the coat tails of the power he drips.

There is a reason Cyrus has stayed King for all these centuries.

No one possesses power and wields it like Cyrus does.

"You will answer Sevan's questions honestly, won't you?" Cyrus says in a low, quiet voice. He places his fore-arms on the table, leaning in.

Terrified, she nods her head.

I don't miss the fact that she never spoke the words.

"You sound Italian," I state. "Is that where you're visiting Austria from?"

"Yes," she says. "My family lives in a small village about two hours from the border."

I nod. Good. She's giving me answers.

"And how many are there in your family?"

This is the part I worry about.

"Just the ten of us," she says. "Our mother, most thought her a miracle, because she conceived so many times. Our father loved her even more because of it. Unfortunately, she died giving birth to my youngest brother."

"And how long ago was that?" Cyrus asks.

"Twenty-two years ago," she says. She seems to be getting a better grip on herself as she provides the answers, and I don't know if that's a good or bad thing. It might mean her mind is clearing, making it easier to lie. "He just Resur-rected two weeks ago. That is the reason our father invited us all here, to Court. To celebrate the immortality of our entire family."

"Are you aware that Lorenzo has other children, here at Court?" I ask. My voice is cold.

Irene nods. "We knew we were not the first family Lorenzo St. Claire had. His previous wives grew old and died. He met our mother later in life."

"With Royal blood, you and your siblings are entitled to certain luxuries," I say. "A life here at Court if you gained favor in the eyes of Cyrus. Or attachments to a House. Why have you lived this life of isolation? Why has Lorenzo kept your existence a secret?"

I see it now. Her confidence once more locks into place. Her eyes are clear of fear. She sits forward. "There are certain expectations when you live at Court. When you are a part of a House. Our father, he wanted us to have a simple, happy life. We've never had to be part of any wars. Never lived a life of suspicion and servitude. He gave us the chance at a normal life."

I mull that over for a moment. Just because I've never heard of another Royal going about life this way doesn't mean it isn't reasonable.

"How many more of you are coming to Roter Himmel?" Cyrus asks.

Her eyes flick to him, and they widen just a bit. And now she knows they are being watched. Listened to.

"We have six other half siblings," she says. But there's something tight about the way she says the words that makes me question if she's telling the truth. "They are traveling from farther away than me and my siblings. They are set to arrive in a few hours."

Cyrus and I look at each other. We're good at holding the

façade. Instead of worried expressions, we hold cold calculation.

I take a deep breath, and look back at Irene. "Like I told you, Roter Himmel is still under lockdown. I expect it will remain so for some time. I am sorry you came all this way for nothing, but I suggest you return home. And that you call your half-siblings and tell them the same."

Her eyes narrow and she sits forward. "It was a long journey, longer for the others in my family. I think we will wait for the day this lockdown is finished."

My hands curl into fists, and her eyes drop down to them. "It might be a long wait."

Her eyes once more flick up to mine. "Trust me, we can be patient."

We stare at one another for a long moment.

I can't read this woman. She seems timid and scared one moment and manipulative and deceitful the next.

"Please let me know when the rest of your siblings arrive," I say. I grab the notepad that was already lying on the table and write down my phone number. "I'd really like to meet the whole family once they've arrived."

"And we would like to get to know you, as well," Irene says, staring at me as a mirthful little smile begins growing on her lips. "Sister."

I stand, shoving my chair back. I won't let her get to me. I won't show an ounce of emotion. Cyrus stands as well, and we take a step toward the door.

"I'm sure you have figured it out by now, you seem like a smart girl," I say as I hesitate in the doorway. "But you're being watched. We have to be careful these days, as we always have been. So don't try anything. Don't leave."

"We wouldn't dream of it," she says as she too stands.

I turn and walk out. Cyrus follows me out into the bright day, sunshades securely in place.

We walk down the road, once more searching the trees for a spy. Thankfully, only a few moments later, the same one darts out onto the road.

"She said there are six more of them that are going to be arriving over the next few hours," I say. "Something makes me think she's lying about the number. Expect more."

The man nods, his lips forming a thin, hard line.

"Don't let them leave the inn," I say. "Don't let them anywhere near the city. We'll be sending more back-up shortly."

He nods and heads back into the trees.

With a look at Cyrus that says we'll discuss this further when out of earshot, we dart off down the road, and back toward Roter Himmel.

CHAPTER 29

I HEAD STRAIGHT FOR THE HEADQUARTERS, CUTTING INTO THE village.

"You didn't show them the army," Cyrus states before we head into the building.

"If they try anything, I'm happy to let them pay the price and see what happens when they walk into all of this," I glower. I go straight for the door, shoving it open to find Dorian, Malachi, and Matthias already gathered.

"What's going on with Lorenzo?" I demand without pleasantries.

Dorian steps forward, folding his arms over his chest. "We've let the rumors go straight to him that some of his children are trying to get into the city. He's been asking questions."

"Like?" I encourage. I'm impatient. Anxious.

"Like how anyone was sure they were his children,"

Dorian continues. "How many of them were there. Where they are now. Who's talked to them."

"Has he said anything else?" I ask. I pace the room, watching Dorian.

"No," Dorian answers. "Though he does seem very agitated. He's been pacing in his cell nonstop since."

I stop, staring at nothing for a long minute.

What does this mean? What's going on?

"No one else thinks it's a coincidence that all these children are showing up soon after he thinks Cyrus is dead, do they?" I say, looking around the room.

"There was time," Malachi says. "There was just over a week between when Cyrus was decapitated to when everyone was brought here for interrogation. He could have told his children anything. They could just see it as an opportunity to integrate into Court without having to get Cyrus' approval."

Hmm. "Maybe," I say, because it's the first logical thought presented so far. "But Irene didn't seem to express interest in staying at Court."

"Lorenzo is most well-known for traveling frequently," Cyrus speaks up. "He hid this family in Italy. Logan was off in the States. Who is to say he doesn't have a dozen families scattered around the globe?"

"For what, though?" I question. "They don't seem to be looking for power, or they easily could have asked for their own House and we probably would have given it to them. Lorenzo has just been laying low here at Court. He hasn't caused any trouble."

I shake my head, feeling frustrated beyond words. "What's his game here?"

My phone buzzes in my back pocket. I pull it out to see a number I don't recognize, but answer it anyway.

"My Queen," a familiar voice immediately says. I recognize it as the spy we'd been talking with. "Another vehicle showed up just moments ago. There are six more yellow-eyed Royals inside."

"That's as many as Irene said were coming," I say, looking up at Cyrus.

"We'll keep an eye on the situation and let you know if anything happens," he says, and then hangs up.

I slip my phone into my pocket, rubbing my temples. "I want Lorenzo's four children who live here at Court under constant watch," I say. "I want them in a secure lock up. And I want Lorenzo to know that we're cracking down on them."

"Of course," Dorian says with a nod.

I don't trust them.

I don't trust anyone.

"Tell me how the interrogations are going," I say. Too much needs to happen too fast. "Please tell me you've caught conspirators."

Matthias actually smiles. "We interrogated a man and a woman this morning. We'd had reason to suspect that they'd let the attacker into the castle. So after leaving them out in the sun for the last six days straight, they were finally ready to talk. They confessed to conspiring with the Born. They were on guard when the man slipped into the castle. They let him right in."

My eyes grow wide. Finally. Something concrete.

"Where are they now?" I demand.

"Under guard in a house," Matthias says with an evil grin. "Four doors down from here."

Without a single word, or without even a breath of his plans, Cyrus turns and stalks out the door, silent and terrifying as the grave.

The rest of us stand frozen, listening, our ears straining.

There's a shout of surprise, and Cyrus' calm but terrifying voice requesting to see the prisoners.

A few moments later there are screams of agony.

I can clearly imagine the painful death they're suffering right now.

"What about the rest of them?" I ask. "Has anyone else confessed to being vampires?"

Malachi looks back to me. "Another seven confessed this morning," he says with disappointment. "In addition to the three last night."

I swear under my breath. That's twenty-five total. More than I feared.

"How close are we to feeling solid?" I ask. "How soon until we will know we can trust everyone else to be on our side? Because I don't know what is going on with Lorenzo's family, but it certainly has me on high alert."

There's a frantic scream, and then the sound of wet, ripping flesh.

My stomach turns.

Even Malachi blanches. He looks toward the building where we all know a lot of carnage is taking place. He swallows once before looking back to me.

"Give me two more days," he says. "We've made progress. I just need two more days."

It's more than I want. More than I feel we have. But shorter than I expected him to say. I nod.

"I need you to send another sixteen Royals to the inn to assist in surveillance," I say. There has to be some more we know we can trust."

Malachi nods.

I hear the sound of a door shutting and footsteps crunching over the cobblestones. A moment later, Cyrus steps back into the building.

Blood is streaked over his entire body. Over his face. Coating his clothes. It drips off his hands. Streaks of it are smeared from his mouth, down his chin and neck.

I look at him, and he looks like a nightmare. He looks like a demon.

But I can't muster even an ounce of horror when I look at him. I don't feel any pity for the people I know he just eviscerated.

"We will return in a few hours," I say. "I want to talk to Lorenzo. Make sure that he hears more of his descendants have arrived. I want him good and agitated when I speak to him."

They all nod in acknowledgement. Cyrus and I walk out of the building, and head back to the castle in the brilliant sunshine, him dripping in blood from head to toe.

We step into our bedroom, and I pace back and forth. Cyrus goes straight for the bathroom. He doesn't shut the door when he turns the water on in the shower. Or when he strips out of his bloody clothes, throwing them in the garbage. Or when he steps into the shower.

I avert an embarrassed but lustful eye, but I'm so

distracted, half of my brain doesn't even notice.

"What do you think is going on, Cyrus?" I ask, still pacing the space at the end of our bed in front of the bathroom door.

I hear water splash, and look over. All I can see is bloody water hitting the glass walls.

"I think that there is much more to Lorenzo than we ever worried to know," he says. I see him reach for the soap and begin scrubbing the blood away.

It's a sight Sevan has seen so many times. Cyrus washing the blood of others from his skin.

But Logan shyly looks away from the fiancé she still hasn't seen completely naked. Not like this. This isn't the way she wants it to be for the first time.

"I think this is some kind of power play," he continues. "He has spread his posterity out, hidden most of them. What he plans to do with them, I don't know the answer to that yet."

I nod. Everything he says makes sense. Of course it's about power. It's about numbers.

"What would you do with them?" I ask, looking over my shoulder at him. "With everything we are already dealing with, what would you do with these people trying to get into the city?"

Cyrus looks over at me, and I meet his dark green eyes. And there's that flicker in them, a darkness there that tells me exactly what he'd do with them.

He'd slaughter them. No more questions.

They're making us feel uneasy. Perhaps unsafe.

He'd kill them all.

"I think you are wise in being cautious," he answers me, because he knows me.

I nod. "I think we need to force them to leave. Now that the interrogation is wrapping up, I think we take those soldiers and make our own show of power. I think we utilize them, and make Lorenzo's descendants leave."

"And what then?" Cyrus asks. "At least with them here, we can watch them. If they leave, they'll go back out and about in the world and we will have no idea if they begin to conspire against us."

I swear. He's right.

I sink onto the bed as Cyrus shuts the water off. I flop onto my back, staring up at the ceiling as wave after wave of pressure crashes down on top of me.

The mattress dips to my right as Cyrus sits on it. He lays beside me, a towel wrapped around his hips, still dripping water everywhere. He brushes hair from my forehead, staring into my eyes.

"You have done incredible things with the resources at hand, and with little to no help, my love," he says gently. "You have held a kingdom thrown into chaos together and kept the beginning of anarchy from rushing to our doors. We will get through this."

He dips down, gently kissing my lips.

I bring my hand to his cheek, drawing him closer into me.

I need him right now.

I need his strength.

I need his wrath.

I need his experience.

I need his support.

Letting my hand slide down, I touch him, feeling he is real. My hand slips down to his neck, where I can feel his pulse. It slides further down, resting over his heart, feeling it beat.

Logan is so hungry, so eager. It's been weeks and months of anticipation. I want this man. I want to be with him. I want him to know every inch of me.

Soon he will. Soon he will be mine.

My Husband.

My partner.

My equal.

The King to my Queen.

"Thank you," I breathe.

He kisses me deeply, his tongue dipping into my mouth, dancing with my own. He shifts on top of me, grinding his hips into mine. I sigh, his mouth trailing to my jaw and then to my neck.

Let the rest of the world go to hell.

My only plans are to stay in this bed with Cyrus, here in heaven.

But on the bed beside me, my phone starts ringing.

With an annoyed growl, Cyrus presses his lips to the base of my throat one last time before pushing off of me and going to the closet.

"What?" I demand, irritated.

"There are another three vehicles that have just arrived, my Queen," the spy reports, undeterred by my tone.

"All children of Lorenzo's?" I demand, sitting straight upright.

"All with the same golden jade eyes," he confirms.

"How many individuals?" I ask as I climb to my feet. I go to the window, slipping on sunshades as I look out into the day. It's busy down in the city, as Malachi and Dorian try to hurry and wrap up things.

"Six in one vehicle, five in each of the others," my spy reports.

Sixteen more descendants.

"Shit," I breathe. "Have my reinforcements arrived yet?"

"Five showed up a few minutes ago, they said more are on the way," he says.

I swear again.

I feel like everything is about to unravel.

"Hold tight," I say. I nod toward Cyrus, who is now fully dressed, and we set off together. "More will be there soon. Please let me know if any others show up."

He makes an affirmative noise and I hang up.

"Thirty-two," I seethe. "There are now *thirty-two* of Lorenzo's children waiting just outside the city."

"No one has ever had so many direct children," Cyrus glowers. "Not our son, not Dorian. Not any other House. I think we know exactly what Lorenzo was doing all that time he was traveling."

"He was gathering mothers, whoring out every night attempting to make children," I say. I feel sick. Because I think of Alivia, totally ignorant as an eighteen-year-old girl, having no idea the sick bastard who tricked her into sleeping with him was doing the same thing every night with a different woman.

I feel sick, because I bear the same eyes as him and all his other bastard children.

CHAPTER 30

ONLY AN HOUR HAS PAST SINCE WE LEFT TOWN, BUT IT'S A flurry of activity. Royals are escorted all over the place by armed soldiers. But when they see Cyrus, he's met with cries of relief and demanding questions.

We can't answer any of them. They deserve to know the answers. But there is no time.

We find Malachi and tell him to bring Lorenzo to us.

In a secluded home close to the castle, we wait.

"I don't want him seeing you," I say. "He can't have gotten word yet that you're alive, the people have only just now seen you. You can watch, but I don't want him seeing you."

Cyrus looks at me, wariness in his eyes. But I see something else: trust. He nods, and slips into the adjoining room, and I don't even hear him breathing.

Thirty seconds later, the door opens, and three guards

march Lorenzo in, guns pointed at his back and head. They shove him down into the seat across the table from me.

He meets my eyes, his own bloodshot, watering against the sun and pain ripping through is brain.

I feel sick. I want to literally tear his eyes from his head, so that my eyes can be my own. So that any tie I have to this man is erased from the earth forever.

"Are you alright, Sevan?" he asks, which makes me even angrier. "This invasion…" He shakes his head. "I can hardly believe that after all these years, it's come to this."

"Cut the caring bullshit," I say. I lean forward. "I don't know how much is a lie and how much is truth, that story about how you met Alivia, about how I was conceived. What I want to know is how many other children you have out there? How many are out there that you've hidden from Court?"

His gaze instantly sobers. His eyes harden. And I see it, one piece at a time chipping off. His façade. His lies.

"I know you've heard, because I asked that the truth be whispered outside your door,'" I say. "I wanted you to know that your children were arriving at Roter Himmel. Tell me, how many more are coming?"

There it is.

A tiny smile begins pulling in the corners of his mouth.

"I don't have time for games, Lorenzo," I say, making my tone icy cold. "I'm a very busy woman these days. It isn't the easiest task, holding all this shit together on my own. There's no time for grief. There's no time to get my head on straight. I don't even have time to breathe. So tell me what is going on, or I will peel your flesh from your bones, right here and now, and I will feed it to the birds piece by piece and make you watch."

His expression does not falter. He holds that smile that makes me want to rip his lips off.

"You know, Court has had no problem pretending like the man who made our population possible didn't exist," Lorenzo says. He places his forearms on the table, leaning in slightly. Goosebumps flash over my skin at the unexpected change of topic to the Blood Father. "There isn't even one single record in this city that bears his name. There are less than a dozen Royal or Born who were alive when he was, and every one of them seem happy to never hear his name spoken again."

My insides grow cold. I feel very still and frozen.

That name echoes inside of my brain, over and over, and with each reverberation, my heart cracks.

"My own parents were taken from me at a young age," Lorenzo continues. "I was alone, left to take care of myself for a long time. It wasn't easy, especially in this town. So I became obsessed with the idea of family very early on. Family is supposed to be there for you. You are supposed to be surrounded by them. They're supposed to help one another, be there to help you achieve your dreams, your goals."

No. I know where this is going.

No.

"But because the Blood Father thought differently than his family, they turned their backs on him," Lorenzo says. He's very calm. And there's a hint of excitement in his voice. "My parents were killed, at Cyrus' own hand."

I sit straighter, as if Lorenzo just slapped me.

He nods. "My father was caught feeding on a human outside of town but didn't realize he was followed back into Roter Himmel. When Cyrus found what had happened, realized how much this human had seen, he executed the human and my father. And my mother..." he shakes his head, his expression bitter and hard. "Even though she was human, she tried to save my father, and it cost her her life as well."

I feel sick.

Because I understand his bitterness, his pain, his anger.

Cyrus doesn't even remember doing this. I asked him what he knew about Lorenzo. If he had remembered killing Lorenzo's parents, he would have told me.

Cyrus took away his family, and doesn't even remember it.

"If we didn't have to hide, if we weren't keeping our existence a secret because Cyrus is afraid, my family wouldn't have been slaughtered," Lorenzo says in a thick voice. "I hated hiding, but I'd seen our kind killed by humans, because we were outnumbered."

My heart beats so fast. My brain is exhausted trying to keep up. To piece all of these pieces together, to figure out what they mean.

"Left alone, I never identified with anyone, my entire life, except with the stories I heard of the Blood Father."

He folds his hands, one over the other, and smiles. "I was surprised as a teenager that there were no books about him. There were only legends. So I took it upon myself to become his historian. I asked, and maybe because they felt sorry for me, others told me what they knew. They told me of his travels around the world. Of him building his family. Of his rise to power. Of how he could influence the world."

"My son was a power-hungry mogul who wanted to take the world for his own," I say. The ice around my heart makes it very difficult to breathe, much less speak. "The world would have descended into constant bloodshed and ruin if he had taken crown over it."

Lorenzo gives a little laugh, his eyes falling to the table. "Probably so," he says. "But you still have to admire him. For spreading our kind. We wouldn't be here if not for him."

Madness. He's spouting madness.

"Why are your children here?" I change directions, leaning forward. My eyes burn into him, begging to find the truth hidden beneath his skin, written on the surface of his scarred, black heart.

"They are here, because after being patient and building my family, after hiding them from knowledge of the Court for the last six hundred years, I have asked them to come. Our time has finally arrived. Now that the King is off the throne."

I feel my face go numb. I sit back in my chair, needing more room to breathe.

There were whisperings at Court. That Royals were not happy with Cyrus. That things needed to change.

"The Royals, Court, the Houses will not mourn that tyrant's death," Lorenzo continues, and I hate that absolute confidence in his voice. "But his absence will throw the world into chaos. You may have experience, Sevan, you may have great ideas. But you and Cyrus? You are only two sides of the same coin. After more than two thousand years, the time for change has finally arrived."

He has gathered his large family so that he can challenge me for the throne. He has brought his own Royal support, people who have claim and say, to back him.

"You want to be King," I say.

Lorenzo smiles. "I want the people to be free. I want them to finally live free of an ages-old tyrant. I only want to help guide them into a new age. Perhaps that is one where all the world knows we exist. Perhaps that is one where the dominion of weak humans comes to an end. But I do believe there is need for an usher."

I shake my head.

I'm filled with horror.

Because I can picture it all. Everything he's described. And with everything that has happened in the last few weeks, I see how easily it could be brought to pass.

"You'll never gain the support of all the Royals," I say, shaking my head. "No, they are not all enamored with Cyrus and the way he's ruled things all these years. But the vast majority do not want to see the world ruined by our kind."

"Oh," Lorenzo says, leaning forward. "But this is my ultimate goal, Sevan." There's a light dancing in his eyes, and I see passion there. I see drive. I see centuries of work. "This is how we change the world. There will be no difference, because in the end, we are all the same. Every single vampire may prove themselves. There will no longer be Born, there will no longer be Royal."

This. *This is* how he wins.

Because for every Royal, there are a hundred Born.

"The division of the Born and the Royals limits our kind," he continues. "I may have resented that I was born a privileged Royal who had to do nothing to prove myself, but it did afford me opportunities. It gave me my chance to find a way to bring our kind back into one family with no division."

The words sound beautiful.

But the reality of it will spell the end for mankind.

"I will stop you," I say, leaning forward. "I will kill you right here, right now."

"And what if I kill you first?" he says. His words are ice cold, but there is a smile on his face.

"Then I will just come back, over and over. I will never stop getting in your way."

All of my insides shake and quiver.

He smiles. "Don't worry, Sevan. Unlike you and Cyrus, I could never kill one of my own children."

A chill works its way down my spine at this monster calling me one of his own children.

My phone rings in my pocket and I instantly whip it out, pressing it to my ear.

"There are more of them!" my spy shouts. He sounds frantic. "Ten more cars just drove up, and I see more down the road."

"How many?" I demand, locking eyes with Lorenzo.

"There have to be sixty-five more here," the spy says. "In addition to the thirty I've already told you about."

One hundred.

There are nearly *one hundred* of Lorenzo's children here at our doorstep.

A sharp ringing sounds in my ears and I set the phone down on the table without hanging up.

"How many?" I whisper. "How many are there?"

Lorenzo, my biological father, looks up at me from beneath his eyelashes. "Four here at court," he begins. "Thirteen in Los Angeles. Twenty-six in Ghana. Twenty-eight in Cairns, Australia." My blood runs chill as I begin totaling up the numbers in my head.

"Thirty-nine in Buenos Aires, Argentina," he just keeps spouting numbers. "Forty-seven in North Korea. Fifty-one in New Delhi. And exactly one hundred between my wives in Italy."

I want to throw up.

Lorenzo has 308 children. Plus me. Plus however many others like me that slipped through his fingers.

There were just over four hundred members here at Court. And I've just shipped nearly twenty-five of them off around the globe.

"How many more are coming here?" I ask. And I can't hide the quake that leaks into my voice.

Once again, Lorenzo smiles. "All of them."

I feel like I'm having a stroke. I swear my brain is flickering in and out. I can't process it all. I can't take it all in. I can't think through all of the implications.

"This doesn't have to be a frightening time, Sevan," he says calmly. He reaches forward, trying to take my hand, but I yank it back, glaring darkly at him. "With your support, this can be such an easy transition. There won't need to be any lives lost."

I shake my head. "Never. I will never, ever support you or

this mutiny."

He makes a sad breathy sound. He shakes his head, and I hate the condescending look in his eyes. "Don't do this, Sevan. The King has fallen. This is the end of an era. The world will change. Do not make yourself vulnerable by standing alone."

The door makes a squealing sound as it swings open.

"Oh, but she is never alone."

It's as if I watch it in slow motion, as Lorenzo's face changes from smug and dark, to shocked and terrified.

It all happens in a fraction of a second. Cyrus is on top of him, fangs bared. They topple one over the other, rolling across the floor.

Cyrus is quicker and stronger. He takes Lorenzo by the front of his shirt, and drags the man out into the sunlight.

I scramble after them, darting out into the street.

But something is wrong when I look around.

There are people, frozen in the streets, their eyes turned toward the mouth of the canyon.

I turn, and my stomach disappears, my hands go numb.

I see them there. Bodies. People. Dozens and dozens of them.

I can't count them all. But I know it instantly.

There are more than a hundred of them.

"The King may have evaded death," Lorenzo says darkly, dangling from Cyrus' grasp. "But the reign of this monarchy is over."

THE END OF BOOK THREE

WANT MORE VAMPIRES?

Can't get enough?

CROWN OF DEATH is part of the
BLOOD DESCENDANTS UNIVERSE

Visit BloodDescendants.com for playlists, maps, news, cast
inspiration, and more!

ABOUT THE AUTHOR

 Keary Taylor is the USA TODAY bestselling author of over twenty novels. She grew up along the foothills of the Rocky Mountains where she started creating imaginary worlds and daring characters who always fell in love. She now splits her time between a tiny island in the Pacific Northwest and Utah, dragging along her husband and their two children. She continues to have an overactive imagination that frequently keeps her up at night.

Made in United States
North Haven, CT
09 May 2024

52344024R00161